The Destruction of the Veil of Islam

Larry Garza

PublishAmerica
Baltimore

First printing

ISBN: 1-4137-1214-2
PUBLISHED BY PUBLISHAMERICA, LLLP
www.publishamerica.com
Baltimore

Printed in the United States of America

DEDICATION

This book with all of its hard work, personal risk of life and fortune, and the more than two million miles of grueling international travel it represents, is dedicated to my greatest adventure of all, the wife of my youth Linda. We married as kids, and we set out into the great unknown of life, traveling across America to my first job. Linda has been my travel companion since that time. She has been an excellent wife and friend. It is only because of the help I have received from God and Linda that I am alive today to tell this story.

Larry and Linda Garza

ACKNOWLEDGEMENTS

I would like to acknowledge some key individuals in my life and this book. They are listed in the chronological order of meeting them.

My Dad, Lauro E. Garza, his life instilled in me an intense love for books, knowledge, and spirituality; I knew him from 1952, the year I was born, until 2001, when he passed from this world.

Alexander my son, he worked very hard in his youth to help me to accomplish my vision. He was born in 1978.

Peter Tan, my first friend in Asia. 1986.

The former John Osteen, who mentored me and shared with me his personal wisdom. 1986

Joseph Prince, my friend of Singapore, who has supported my efforts from the beginning. 1988

U Saw Junior, Karen Guerilla Commander in Burma, who guarded my life many times. 1988

Chuck and Jo Tucker, they stood with me through thick and thin. 1989

Nakorn Weschpaporn, gave me his home in Thailand to use as a base for all of Asia. 1989

Dr. Guo Hai my friend who opened the door to all of China. 1990

Benin, my amazing Sri Lankan coordinator, he proved to be an invaluable help. 1990

Manlay Bayar, my friend in Mongolia. 1991

Buzzy Sutherlin, my friend in Arkansas, he understands who I am and what I am doing. 1992

Zam Refai, my good Moslem friend from Sri Lanka, I love him greatly because of the great respect he has extended me. 1992

John Hu, my essential companion who guided me in the remote regions of China, I love him like a brother. 1993

Mashrab, my Moslem host in Uzbekistan. 1994

Ali Akbar, my Moslem friend, I love him like a brother; he protected me across Pakistan along the Afghanistan border three times. 1997

Oleg Panushkin, he opened Kyrghyzstan to me with his official invitation. 1996

Mehran, a Moslem intellectual who helped me get out of Iran safely when I was severely injured. 1998

Marie Carriker, my dedicated secretary, she has been a big help with this book.

Table of Contents

Chapter 1
Visions of Paradise:
Bukhara, Uzbekistan 1995

"Fortune is not on the side of the faint-hearted."
Sophocles

"You've got to make something happen."
Larry Garza

I was on the fringes of the Kyzyl Kum desert; men with fur hats, robes, and daggers prominently displayed, thronged around us. The smelly smoke of burning lamb fat from the many greasy kebab sticks being grilled, hung in the air like the bad smog of Indonesia. The discordant tones of different Asiatic languages struck my ears in so indiscernible a manner that I could not tell whether they were engaged in arguments or intense bargaining.

I felt like we had gone back in time to some Moslem dream of a desert trade city. In reality that is exactly what Bukhara had been. For centuries it was the halfway point on the Old Silk Road. Marco Polo had been here and so had many other renowned explorers.

The local Islamic rulers known as Emirs became famous for their arbitrary and exceedingly cruel whims. The slightest provocation of the Emir would result in the unfortunate person being thrown into the local combination cesspool/dungeon famous for its menagerie of reptiles and spiders. This happened to two British officers who came offering treaty with England. If you weren't Moslem upon entering the city you became one or died. The stalwart Englishmen refused the choice, were imprisoned, and then killed. There still remains to this day the very tall tower in the center of the city from which many of the condemned were flung to their deaths on the pavement below.

It was 1995, and I was in the exotic bazaar of Bukhara, Uzbekistan with my friend Robert Dowdy. When initially I had announced my plans to visit this holy city of Islam in Central Asia, Robert Dowdy felt adamant he was to accompany me. That day in the bazaar I thought I could see a twinge of regret in his face. Now that we were here, maybe he wasn't so sure. That morning, after breakfast in our hotel, I told him, "Now we've got to make something happen!" This is how we had come to venture out into the oriental bazaar filled with colorful characters. Rigid Soviet Stalinism intertwined with the vicious Islamic past to produce an atmosphere of heavy repression that made it hard to breath easy anywhere in Uzbekistan. The mission we were on didn't make it any easier. The last man caught with the banned videos we were carrying had his hands and feet burned to the point of uselessness by the local authorities.

Suddenly as the crowd pressed in around us, two men punched us solidly in our midsections. The blows were enough to hurt but not quite enough to make one bowl over. Robert tensely asked me, "What do we do?"

I grunted, "Don't hit back, we're outnumbered!" The knowledge of the innumerable daggers that surrounded us quenched any thoughts I had of reprisal.

We walked quickly through the melee and we entered the calm of a small store. Safely inside, I began to interact with the people and was surprised to find a young man who could speak some elementary English. I used my need of a hat to fuel the discussion. Americans being unknown in these parts, he was keenly interested in our conversation and the opportunity to practice English.

Our visit to Bukhara coincided with Ramadan, a month long Moslem religious fast. The daily main event of Ramadan occurs each evening. After the sun sets, and the moon is sighted, the Imam declares the people can eat until sunrise. Not even water is allowed during the day!

The city was an ancient center of many Islamic madressahs, a type of Islamic seminary for religious instruction. Bukhara was said to be such a great place of learning that Islamic holy men of old said that light went up, not down in the city!

The age of Stalinism and Soviet occupation had brought many Russians to Bukhara. So not every one was observing the Ramadan. It was important to discern the Russians from the Moslems. I noted that the owner wore a Haji skullcap under his fur hat. It was obvious he was an ardent Moslem.

Inside their store I spied a very small boy about four or five years of age. He caught my eye because he was so cute. He was dressed as an exact miniature of the adult men in the area. I patted him on the head and asked the man interpreting whose son he was and if I could give him some chewing gum. It turned out he was the son of the proprietor who looked very pleased at the attention his son was receiving.

Returning to my search for a Karakul hat I was disappointed when the proprietor said he didn't have one. The Bukhara region is famous for its lamb's wool, called Karakul, which is made into hats and other items of clothing.

As I spoke with the local people in the store, the owner, a man named Mashrab turned to me and invited Robert and I to break the daily fast with a sacrifice and Iftar dinner that evening! Mashrab informed us he was a member of the Tajik tribe.

Because of my research, I knew the honor his invitation conferred. Among the true practicing Moslems of Asia it is almost unknown for them to invite a Christian or Jew to eat at their home. To do so, according to the tribal laws of hospitality, makes the host responsible for his guest's safety. It is also a form of a covenant, whereby the guest and host enter into a special relationship. Even ardent enemies respect the law of hospitality and would never attack another's guest. I quickly accepted. He gave us directions and told us to come after sundown.

As we walked up to the residence on the outskirts of Bukhara the next night, it was obvious that this was a rich man's house. Though drab on the outside, the house was built on the Oriental theme of many rooms built around a main courtyard. After being admitted by a guard into the courtyard, we followed him to our host's place of dinner.

Sneaking a glance into an open window, my eyes were rewarded with a scene from what Moslems would think to be Mohammed's Paradise. The reaction of the occupants made obvious that I had laid my eyes on the forbidden.

Women clad in richly decorated robes sat on the floor of a room. Their veils hanging loosely to one side, revealed their faces. They ate sumptuously from the heaps of foods on large platters.

The room had only a little furniture, yet the decor rivaled that of an Emirs palace. Oriental silk fabrics with raised patterns in gold and silver covered the walls. Very large, ornate carpets covered every bit of floor space. My eyes reeled from the vision of paradise.

We walked into a doorway just as a large ram was being brought from the outside into the center of the courtyard.

Our host greeted us and brought us into a western style room with a table and chairs. He told Robert Dowdy and I that a ram was being sacrificed for the Iftar dinner. We made small talk until a man brought a platter with the roasted heart, and set it on the table. A simply dressed elderly matriarch came in and prayed while wiping her face with both hands, as was their custom in prayer.

Together we ate the heart of the sacrificed ram. The tough flesh, though well cooked, tasted of blood rich tissue accented by the unmistakable strong mutton flavor. Fresh unleavened bread baked in rounds called Naan was brought in.

Our host Mashrab took an entire Naan, and standing by my place at the table ceremoniously broke it in half, carefully placing one half on each side of my plate. He was making covenant with me!

My spirit filled with joy! I had arrived in this ancient stronghold of Islam on a mission knowing no one. Now an obviously wealthy Moslem merchant of the city was extending the Quranic law of hospitality and friendship to me. I had his protection! I ate the freshly grilled flesh of the ram with relish at my good fortune.

I was presented with a fine Karakul hat as a gift at our meal. None of the beautifully attired women I had seen on entering the courtyard ever came into the room. As we drank tea I spoke freely of my life and mission. If disturbed by my infidel faith they never let on. I asked if I could pray a blessing over them all. They agreed, bringing even the matriarch back into the room for my prayer. Standing, I laid hands on their foreheads praying for the several men and the mother. I told them I had a special gift, but I wanted to present it to them at a dinner the next evening at my hotel, the Hotel Bukhara. They agreed to my reciprocal hospitality.

We were in deep now! What I planned to do had no turning back to it. Once I presented them with the video and pamphlets, if they chose to, they could turn me into the local authorities. Or, just their anger could cause them to turn violent and attack us. I was counting on their salt covenant, enacted over a meal and the Islamic law of hospitality to keep us safe.

That next day waiting for my Moslem guests, I tried to reassure myself with the memory of Dr. Joseph Wolff, an adventurer who traveled this region of the world in the nineteenth century. I specifically remembered reading that his life had been spared because he reminded his Moslem captors of their law of hospitality. I felt that divine providence was with us and that I had been supernaturally provided with protection. The next night I hosted the men of the family at our hotel for dinner and presented them with a video and several pamphlets. When they left, I turned to Robert and said, "There is no turning back now!"

That night, we gathered for a final dinner. The atmosphere was very tense as Mashrab and his companions ate. Hardly anyone spoke.

He then asked me in very guttural and accusatory tone, "Video, Muslim?"

"No," I replied and I shared very freely about my life and purposes. He listened politely but not enthusiastically. Our dinner came to a courteous but quick end.

The next day we left Bukhara in a car headed for Samarkand. Mixed emotions of relief, joy, and the excitement of a great adventure flooded my life. I had been able to accomplish my purpose in this ancient Moslem stronghold, and I was alive and well!

You probably are asking, how did I get involved in such an exotic adventure and what was my mission? At one time I worked for the world's largest oil company and lived an American suburban life. What were the reasons and events that led me to live such high adventure? **The answer is complex and detailed. It is an amazing story that has to do with the final events of civilization and my personal search for the truth. Our incursion into Uzbekistan was part of a deliberate plan on my behalf to bring the truth to The Islamic Central Asian Republics.**

My motivation to go to Bukhara without introduction or contact was an inspiration from the life of Sir Francis Richard Burton. The actual itinerary came from historical journals of the great explorers of Asia. I read the biography of Sir Francis Richard Burton, a powerful yet controversial figure of the nineteenth century. He was a fantastic philologist speaking twenty-six languages fluently! He was also one of the best swordsmen of his time, a great author, and adventurer. He explored Africa and was one of only thirteen Europeans able to penetrate Mecca, Saudi Arabia.

This last venture, being extremely hazardous, he disguised himself as a Moslem speaking only Arabic and entered the city of Mecca on what is known as the Moslem Hajji or Holy pilgrimage. It came as a revelation to me that if he could do these things, so could I. Sir Francis Richard Burton became the governor of Damascus, Syria and was studying an esoteric Moslem sect called the Shazlis. It was at this time that Jesus Christ appeared to a group of these Shazlis Moslems that were praying and eventually twenty-five thousand converted to Christianity! This event created a violent upheaval in Damascus with great persecution for the converts. Sir Burton came to their rescue.

It was in the biography of Sir Burton, written by Edward Rice that I read this account and I became greatly inspired. I knew that if I would just take on the task of going to these Moslem countries that a supernatural miracle awaited me to help me on my mission. This is how I came to target Bukhara, Uzbekistan and travel across that country.

It has been my good fortune to experience many episodes in exotic and remote areas of the world. I have crossed the Western branch of the Himalayas known as the Karakorum at sixteen thousand five hundred feet from Pakistan into China several times. I journeyed across China two thousand five hundred miles by jeep, retracing Marco Polo's steps. My mission has taken me two thousand one hundred miles across Tibet at altitudes of sixteen thousand to eighteen thousand feet. I've traveled the highest mountains of the world; the Himalaya of Tibet, the Pamirs of Kyrghystan, the Tian Shan and Kunlun Shan of China, and many others as well. My trips have taken me to Syria, Iran, Egypt, Turkey, Vietnam, Cambodia, Laos, Pakistan, Mongolia, Turkmenistan, and many other exotic places.

The great deserts, jungles, and mountains of the world have been my stomping grounds. But it has not been adventure that drove me to these places. It was a specific knowledge shared by men like Sir Isaac Newton and Admiral Christopher Columbus that fueled my itineraries. The lives of great explorers like Dr. Roy Chapman Andrews, the aforementioned Sir Francis Richard Burton, Sir Aurel Stein, Sven Hedin, and Nikolay Przhevalsky, provided strategy and geographical routes.

Christian pioneers like Dr. David Livingstone, Henry Morton Stanley, and General Chinese"Charles" Gordon helped to set my course spiritually, and intellectually.

My purpose was not travel or adventure; I was a messenger of the final scenario that will bring the civilizations of the world into a final conflict in the twenty-first century.

You will find in the following narrative an explanation of the current global conflict, why I say the power of Islam is being destroyed, and amazing accounts of my personal experience.

January 1998 was supposed to be another year of my global travels working in Burma, Sri Lanka, Pakistan and other nations when there suddenly occurred an interruption in my "normal" schedule. It came totally out of the blue, an unexpected direction for my life that would change everything.

I began to receive a series of revelations that were so intense that they would absorb me for many hours every day. For about two months my time was spent in ardent study. I was obsessed with Archeology, Anthropology, History, and Eschatology. The world of ecstatic spiritual states became fused with equally strenuous mental activity. While this was not my first time to take a period of study on these subjects, the duration and intensity of research exceeded all my previous sessions. It would be accurately descriptive to say that I experienced a divine obsession with the purposes and forces of history.

It was during this time that I began to see and understand the current world scenario of 2001. It became intuitively apparent to me that the greatest conflict the world had ever seen was about to occur. The key participants in this violent drama were to be the Moslems, the United States, and the Christians of the world.

> **•The impending attacks of Islamic terrorists on the United States became evident to me.**
>
> **•New coalitions of world super powers were revealed. I was able to anticipate the unexpected and sudden rise of former empires of the ancient world.**
>
> **•O.P.E.C. and the Arab world were to be humbled. The Petro-dollar would crash and burn.**
>
> **•Iraq was to be an instrument of horror and**

rampage to its neighbors and the world.
•Iran was to become an ally of the United States.
•I spoke of anthrax, germ warfare, atomic bombs
and the destruction of the World Trade Center.
•Emphatically I forewarned of the imminent
disappearance of long established global economic
and political hierarchies.
•Different types of world cataclysmic events were
the subjects of my teachings.

Several thousand people heard me foretell these events. As of April 2002 most of these prophecies are facts, but the Spirit of God had me speak them out in 1998 three years before they happened. I was so concerned that I rented the auditorium at the Red Lion Hotel in Houston, Texas for public announcement and even advertised on television. My wife, Linda, and I appeared on a Channel 22 T.V. interview program with the late Eldred Thomas. On this program I publicly declared that Jesus was taking a harvest from the Moslem world and then the end would come.

My time of applied concentration culminated in a great adventure to the Islamic Republic of Iran. My wife and I traveled across the nation visiting Biblical archaeological sites and mingling with the people. The main goal of our itinerary was to visit the ruins of the ancient citadel of Susa. The fascination that drove us to one of the most dangerous places in the world for an American was rooted in events that transpired in ancient history. Those historical events became relevant to me in modern history. I was caught up in the forces and purposes of history that had been revealed when civilization was brand new. In fact, there in that area of the world the end of our era was shown from the very beginning of time.

True history can only be said to begin with writing. Before writing came into being the documentation of eras and events is only hypothetical. Only when human witnesses began to write, did accurate time measurement begin. It was in this area of the world that writing and our civilization began.

In Susa, Iran, about twenty-five hundred years ago, one of history's most accurate and controversial predictions took place. The rise and fall of all empires was foretold. It was so precise that from then until now it has incited arguments as well as interest.

What took place there obsessed the greatest scientific genius the world has ever seen, Sir Isaac Newton. The same man who gave us all the basic laws of physics spent his life from the age of twelve until his death, absorbed in the understanding and analysis of those predictions. He wrote an explanation of the ancient prophecy from Susa and the Mesopotamian world. I own an inexpensive copy of the edition that was in the library of President Thomas Jefferson. Its title is, *Observations Upon the Prophecies Of Daniel and the Apocalypse of St. John*, by Sir Isaac Newton.

Linda and I just had to go there and stand in Susa at the place where the prophet Daniel said, "IN the third year of the reign of Belshazzar the king a vision appeared to me, Daniel, subsequent to the one which appeared to me previously. And I looked in the vision, and it came about while I was looking, that I was in the citadel of Susa, which is in the province of Elam; and I looked in the vision, and I myself was beside the Ulai Canal."

During my period of intense revelation I saw that the prophetic vision given to Daniel was a key to understanding the events of our time. Many people do not know that the tomb of Daniel is there, right on the spot where he saw himself in the vision. He is buried on the banks of the Ulai River in Susa.

Some modern day scholars do not believe that the tomb of Daniel is still existent from that ancient world. They think that his tomb is a legend rather than based on historical fact.

However, there are some amazing points that we must first consider. **Whether Daniel is buried there or not does not alter the fact that this is the place where he said the revelation of all times and civilizations was given and explained to him.**

We must also consider the amazing and really miraculous

archaeological evidence discovered in the last one hundred and fifty years.

Susa is also the location of another famous account, that of King Xerxes and Queen Esther.

For generations the local inhabitants spoke of the area as the site of Susa, yet there was no archaeological proof.

In the early 1800s, many educated people from Christian civilization thought that places like Susa, Nineveh, and Babylon were historical fiction. The Bible stories of those places were thought to be moral stories with no actual history behind them. At that time, the Books of Daniel, Jonah, and Esther as represented in the Bible had no historical authenticity, even though the people of Iran and Iraq lived in the light of this past as a part of their present reality.

If you went to Iraq today and asked those dwelling along the Euphrates, "Who was your founding father?" They would reply, "Nimrod!" Just as the account of Genesis chapter ten says.

The educated people of the world thought the beliefs of the local people were the myths and fables of the region. It is very difficult for the western mind to understand cities where people have lived continuously for thousands of years. The frame of reference in those places is much like our neighborhoods, but with a memory of generations. When someone stops and asks you as you stand in your driveway, "Is there a restaurant near here?" Your mind flashes to the one close by that was built in the last year. In the ancient world their frame of reference runs into thousands of years, not just the last year or two! As they stand by their flocks and you ask who is responsible for the ruins of a great city on the hilltop nearby, their mind flashes to what their family has always known, "it was Nimrod."

The Prophet Daniel said that he was instructed to seal up the knowledge given to him until a special time would come that would be marked by a dramatic global lifestyle. "But as for you, Daniel, conceal these words and seal up the book until the end of time; many will go back and forth, and knowledge will increase." (Daniel 12:3) God hid from the sophisticated and educated what was a historical reality to the simple shepherds of Iraq!

A little more than a one hundred and fifty years ago an Englishman named Henry Austen Layard unearthed Nineveh. Thirty-six years later a French couple, the Dielafoys, found the palace of Queen Esther at Susa. Fourteen years after the Dielafoy discovery, a German team found Babylon.

These events coincide with the birth of our modern era when knowledge has, as Daniel prophesied, "greatly increase" and people can easily "go back and forth" to any place in the earth.

Reading the accounts of these discoveries fueled my mental and spiritual life. Even though I believe in the Holy Texts bound together in the book called the Bible, scientific and historical evidence makes the events of those ancient narratives conclusive for me. Have you ever considered this fact? The issues and places that are the focus of God's attention in those age-old manuscripts, still obsess the world today! Babylon has become a suburb of Baghdad. Nineveh is a part of Mosul. Jerusalem is both a new and old city. Susa is now part of Iran. All these ancient cities still run the world directly or indirectly.

It is an obvious proof many wish to overlook that the God of the Bible is still running the world. This fact has always fascinated me! Isaiah, Jeremiah, and Daniel are still relevant commentators on world events. In fact, careful reading of their remarks will reveal a pattern of repetitious cycles of history that can be counted on to re-fulfill themselves.

Assyria hated Israel, invaded and conquered her. Iraq has replaced old Assyria on today's modern map. Iraqis still hate Israel and are still trying to invade her. Babylon terrorized its world with weapons of destruction. Babylon has become Baghdad today and the world is still intimidated by its arsenal. Twenty-six hundred years ago a fierce King lived in Babylon named Nebuchadnezzar who would often capriciously kill his own counselors on the slightest whim. Until recently, there was a vicious, fierce King named Saddam Hussein, who on a whim would kill his advisors. He murdered his own son-in-law for displeasing him!

Today we find ourselves still living in the world of the Bible and what the prophets predicted is still trustworthy.

In the utterances of the Prophet Isaiah we find one of those re-fulfilling statements: "And it will come about in that day, that the Lord will start His threshing from the flowing stream of the Euphrates to the brook of Egypt; and you will be gathered up one by one, O sons of Israel. It will come about also in that day that a great trumpet will be blown; and those who were perishing in the land of Assyria and who were scattered in the land of Egypt will come and worship the Lord in the holy mountain at Jerusalem." In this passage Isaiah said the God of the Bible would harvest His people from the River Euphrates to the land of Egypt. God has already fulfilled these oracles more than once.

After the conquest of Babylon by the Medo-Persian King Cyrus in 539 B.C., the Jews were set free from all the empire to return to Jerusalem. In the first six centuries after the birth of Jesus Christ, many people became Christians in Syria, Egypt, Arabia, Turkey, Iraq, and Iran. In the last century when the formation of the state of Israel took place, a physical harvest was taken from all over the world. They came to Mount Zion especially from the areas mentioned above because of Islamic persecution. It is only logical that He will do it again. Better yet, He will reap His harvest both spiritually and physically.

There is a big problem confronting the spiritual harvest. All the governments of that region are Moslem and they forbid any spiritual activity outside their narrow world view. In places like Iran for a Moslem to convert is death. In Egypt and Iraq Christians are persecuted and murdered. A non-Moslem cannot testify in a court of law in many Islamic nations.

These are all very intense methods of keeping up a wall so nothing spiritually positive can occur. Strategies include the diabolical and illegal methods of violent attacks. As a parallel you can think in terms of the infamous Iron Curtain of the Communists.

Instead of an iron curtain, we now have the Veil of Islam.
God was not stopped by the violence of Nebuchadnezzar nor will He be denied His purposes today. It is plain to see that in order to complete His plans according to predictions, He will remove the Veil of Islam. Nothing is impossible with God! He will take a harvest from people who have been denied any knowledge of Him.

This is a very brief synopsis of the knowledge and events that prepared us for the trip to Iran. The journey to Iran would take us to the very center of God's vision and plan given to Daniel for the very last days of planet Earth. In the chapters ahead I will fill in the blanks.

Armed with this knowledge and certainty of God's Final Plan, Linda and I headed for the great adventure before us in ancient Persia. The trip to Iran was to be more than a journey. It became a pilgrimage.

The Tomb of Queen Esther the wife of King Xerxes located
in Hamadan, Iran

Standing in front of the Tomb of the Prophet Daniel

Chapter 2
The Royal Road of God:
2,100 Miles Across Iran

"I shall be telling this with a sigh
Somewhere ages and ages hence:
Two roads diverged in a wood, and I
I took the one less traveled by,
And that has made all the difference."
                                    Robert Frost

"My plans were to use the time worn historic highways of the
old world empires, the Royal Road and the Old Silk Route. Along
these roads God traveled by way of prophets, soldiers,
missionaries, and traders."
                                    Larry Garza

In March of 1998, we applied for visas to Iran. There was no diplomatic relationship between the United States and The Islamic Republic of Iran, so we submitted our applications to the Iranian Interest section of the Pakistani Embassy. We gave as the official reason for our visit an archaeological tour of the nation. We knew it would take a miracle to obtain the visas.

Our visas to visit Iran were not granted until 4:00 P.M. on the

Friday before our departure, at almost the very last possible minute. We faced the tense expectation of our dangerous destination. On top of that was added the stress of wondering why we were kept waiting to the last moment.

Linda had insisted on going with me because no man we knew would. Along with all my other cares, I had added the weight of responsibility for taking my wife into a hostile place, rife with potential for violence. She would have to dress in compliance with Iranian Shar'ia law, which meant the Moslem garb with head covering, or a ridiculous bulky raincoat with a scarf at all times.

Travel arrangements within Iran had to be made via a tour company in Canada. The Canadian company usually set up travel for Iranians who lived in the U.S. and were going home to visit. I don't know how many native Americans if any had visited Iran from 1979 to 1998, but I can assure you visits by Americans were extremely rare.

The American embassy had been stormed and our consular officials were taken hostage for 444 days during the Carter Administration. Travel to Iran had been extremely dangerous for Americans. In the establishment of the "Islamic Republic," Christians had been persecuted and vehemently murdered.

Speaking the message of Jesus Christ or converting to it was punishable by death. So, we had two strikes against us going in: American citizenship and our Christian faith. I really did not want to contemplate the consequences of a third strike!

It is very difficult to explain the force compelling us to go to Susa where the revelation of all time had been given to the visionary Daniel. We were drawn to the ancient land of Persia by the history of what God had done and what the prophecies said He was going to do.

We flew into Tehran from Dubai on Emirate Airlines, an air carrier that uses a lot of English, Australians and other non-Moslem nationalities as pilots and attendants.

As the airplane taxied up to the arrival terminal at Tehran airport, the atmosphere in the cabin seemed to thicken with pressure.

Passengers who had been talking and chatting amicably suddenly got very quiet.

Just before the door opened the female flight attendants went to the back of the cabin. I asked one of them, "What is the matter?"

The chief stewardess answered me with a sardonic smile, "We have been warned not to allow ourselves to be seen by the ground crew or any one else because of our western attire. So we have to be as far away from the door as possible!" Her comments made every western woman on the plane nervously adjust their scarves and baggy, fully buttoned raincoats. Those in Moslem garb serenely awaited the opening of the cabin door.

Entering the main arrival hall we could see a huge banner stating, "Palestine the First International Islamic Issue."

Fortunately, we cleared immigration and customs after a brief search. Outside, our guide and driver were waiting. The guide came up, introduced himself and greeted Linda and I by asking what our plans were.

I explained to him the thousand or more mile route that would take us on a big loop through the western half of Iran. My plans were to use the time worn historic highways of the old world empires, the Royal Road and the Old Silk Route.

Along these roads, God traveled by way of prophets, soldiers, missionaries, and traders.

All types of travelers had spread the Word of God in the now dim past.

Apostles and Prophets had ridden these roads freely. Many times they traveled against their will in forced relocations.

The loop I planned would take us west of Tehran to Hamadan, the age-old summer residence of the Persian Kings. Hamadan with its elevation, was an escape from the incredible summer heats of Susa located next to the Persian Gulf. Tradition said that Queen Esther and her uncle Mordecai were buried there in Hamadan.

We planned to enter the Zagros mountain range west of Hamadan on the highway which connected Babylon, where a very famous mountain is located that offers a great breakthrough in understanding the ancient world.

Behistun is a precipitous rock that stood for millennia there outside Hamadan. On this mountain, about three hundred feet up on its cliff wall, stood inscribed an inscription. It was an account of the victories of Darius the Great written about five hundred years before Christ and it was recorded in the cuneiforms of the three arcane languages; Babylonian, Old Persian, and Elamite. One of the world's greatest archaeological triumphs occurred in the mid 1800's when these antiquities were translated making it possible to read the cuneiform tablets of Mesopotamia and Persia. Equally important it helped to vindicate Bible history.

Sir Henry Creswicke Rawlinson hung from the top of the mountain face in a small swing and meticulously copied the strange writing. Hanging dangerously from the side of the mountain, it took him several years just to copy the cuneiform symbols. Then he was to work on their translation for years. He was able to accomplish it with the help of an Irish Pastor named Edward Hincks. Thank God for the men who have had the vision to devote themselves to causes that have given the world priceless information.

The life stories of these great people reveal the handiwork of the God of the Bible at work in motivating and inspiring mankind. They have been instruments of divine revelation just like the prophets. Daniel said in the 12th chapter of the book of his visions, "In the last days knowledge would increase." The increase of knowledge would be necessary for the final events of civilization to be understood. The truth is that in the last one hundred fifty years God has released the historical and scientific information for us to know very accurately that the prophecies, visions, and oracles of the Bible are being quickly completed. God's Final Plan is in effect.

To see the Behistun inscriptions was to experience the milestone that connected the past with the present and helped to explain it.

The Behistun inscription stands on a very famous route that connected Hamadan with the famous Royal Road of the Persian Empire. The Royal Road ran from Susa on the Persian Gulf to Izmir in modern Turkey on the Aegean Sea with many minor branches leading to centers of civilization.

People first started using the Royal Road in about 3500 B.C. Pilgrims, prophets, soldiers, missionaries, and traders have traveled this way for more than five thousand years! Even the children of Israel, when they traveled to Babylon, would first go north and join the Royal Road. Nebuchadnezzar used it to conquer Jerusalem. Daniel, Ezra, Nehemiah, and many others traveled along it as well. Some walked reluctantly as they went, others ran down the road with joy.

From Hamadan we planned travel to Kermanshah on the Iraqi border where we would turn south to travel along Iraq's periphery to Susa, situated in Southwestern Iran. This is the area known in history and the Bible as the province of Elam. The people of Elam were taken captive by the Assyrians and relocated to Israel. There were Jews from Elam on pilgrimage in Jerusalem on the Day of Pentecost who converted to Christianity and returned to Southwestern Iran with the witness of the Resurrection. Susa was the capital of Elam and the later Persian Empire.

According to tradition, it was to Susa that Cyrus the Medo-Persian King brought the Seer Daniel after his conquest of the city Babylon about two hundred sixty miles away. We know that Daniel didn't go home to Jerusalem with the exodus from Babylon. Obviously his skills were considered too valuable by King Cyrus, as they had been by King Nebuchadnezzar of Babylon.

Even though the book of Daniel starts off in Babylon, in the eighth chapter he speaks from the location of the banks of the Ulai River in Susa. Daniel doesn't tell us he was taken to Susa, but he does tell us that the vision of all empires came to him there in the province of Elam. Some scholars believe Daniel spent his old age in Susa and that he is buried there. On the side of the Ulai river is a monument that claims to be his tomb.

From Susa we would travel south to Ahwaz, a great oil center that had experienced Iraqi bombardment in the Iranian-Iraqi war.

From Ahwaz we would turn east to cross over the Zagros mountains and journey to Shiraz. Shiraz is another city of rich history but its time of importance was of a later date than that of the Prophets Isaiah or Daniel.

Northeast of Shiraz towards Tehran, I planned to visit two fantastic places, Pasargadae and Persepolis. Pasargadae had been the first capital of the Persians. Cyrus the Great, founder of the Persian dynasty known as the Achaemaneans that ruled Persia for more than two hundred years, was buried there. Cyrus had conquered Babylon, set the Jews free, and paid for the rebuilding of the temple in Jerusalem. The tomb of Cyrus the Great is at Pasargadae. Alexander the Great came to the tomb there and made homage more than two thousand years ago. Cyrus is mentioned by name in the 43rd chapter of Isaiah about one hundred fifty years before he was born as the Prophet predicted his taking Babylon. Persepolis was later a government center built by Darius the Great.

These people and places figured prominently in the prophecies and events of the Bible and in the formation of our modern civilization. The undiscerning person would look at these locations and think they were dusty and of no relevance to modern life. Actually they are keys to understanding the future as well as the past.

Revelation knowledge had brought the spiritual and temporal worlds together for me. To think that my interest in these places or events was archaeological or historical is to misunderstand their true importance. The events, people, and places from the Near East, Mesopotamia, and Persia are proof of the predictions of the Holy Texts of the Old Covenant.

Think of it this way. If I have made predictions and they are 80% fulfilled, then you can be sure the 20% unfulfilled are certain. So it is with Daniel, Isaiah, and Jeremiah, 80% of what they predicted has happened. I am excited about the 20% that is occurring now. History is coming to a dramatic climax that much of the world does not properly anticipate.

From Shiraz to Isfahan we embarked on a branch of another very old route, the Silk Road. The camel caravan stop of Isfahan was the next significant point on our journey with its great buildings of the early Moslem era. From there we would proceed north through the Ultra-fundamentalist Moslem city of Qom and back to Tehran.

When I had explained my desired itinerary to the Iranian translator and guide, he told me that he thought I knew exactly where I wanted to go and that he was along to help me. The driver was a pleasant, smiling man named Mohammed who drove a small make of Iranian car known as the Paykan.

That first night we spent in Tehran, Linda and I had our hearts swirling with many different emotions. Uncertainty and excitement mixed together to make for a night of restless sleep. The next day we got on the road to Hamadan. I've traveled across the entire continent of Asia by road and I know that with God it doesn't take long for exciting things to start happening. Of course many times he uses us as the catalysts.

My guide was college educated, and spoke five languages. He was schooled as a tour operator for Iran but he didn't know that the tombs of Esther and Mordecai were located in Hamadan. There isn't any concrete factual evidence for Esther and Mordecai being buried in Hamadan but it did make historical sense. Queen Esther's husband is called Ahasuerus in the book titled by her name. He is very well known in history as King Xerxes. This is the same Xerxes that took with him an army of one million Persians to fight against the Greeks. Apparently our guide had no previous knowledge of Queen Esther or Mordecai before our meeting. As is done the world over by travelers, he just asked for the location of the tombs from the locals we encountered when we arrived in Hamadan. I will simply refer to him as "our guide" to protect his identity. Due to the events that transpired on our journey it could be very dangerous for him to be known in Iran.

The location of the tomb was not what I expected. The place didn't look like a museum or shrine. Instead there was a huge wall that seemed to run the perimeter of a large city block. We got down

31

from our car, knocked at a big iron gate and a scruffy looking watchman appeared. He stood on the top of the wall and loudly shouted in Farsi, trying his best to make us leave. I ignored him and circled around the perimeter looking for another entrance. Curiously there were Stars of David in steel design all around the top of the wall. However someone had sawn off one tip of every star so as to make them pentagons. But they had been there so long you could see the less weathered area exposed by the removed tips. The guide ran around from the front main gate where he had stayed and called me, gesturing emphatically. I came back around to the front and standing there was a man who was a caricature of old world looks. His countenance was of a dark complexion with a prominent nose and he was wearing a long frock coat.

My guide told us as we entered the compound that this was a Synagogue and that the dark complexioned man was the Rabbi!

Linda and I were totally shocked!

"Is Esther's tomb here we asked?" When the guide spoke our question to him in Persian he nodded his head affirmatively. We entered a large courtyard and he took us to a section where many candles had been lit. He told us through our translator they had just finished celebrating the feast of Purim from the Book of Esther. He then led us over to an old, but essentially featureless building that had a low door. Stooping low as we entered, it was like passing into another world. Linda and I knew that we had passed into a special sanctuary, not because of the furniture, but because of the atmosphere in the room. There was a divine presence obvious in here but not discernable from the outside.

We saw pictures of Moses and a plaque with the ten commandments in Hebrew on the wall. I asked the Rabbi through my guide, "How long has this synagogue been here?" He replied immediately, "Since the time of Daniel."

An amazing feeling swept over Linda and I! A sense of awe and veneration toward God overcame us. I fought back tears and Linda just let them flow. Curiously the rabbi just looked back at us with a totally impassive face. To be in a place of such historical magnitude is impossible to properly describe. In such a moment one feels a direct connection with the past. It is as if Daniel and Esther were in the room with us and we were a continuing part of what they were doing. My wife began to try to explain to him. He stood patiently listening with that same expressionless face.

Highly inspired, Linda began to speak to him about the resurrection of Jesus Christ and how it had changed our lives.

Unsympathetically, the guide interrupted her with the question, "Are you trying to change his religion?" An ominous feeling tried to interrupt the glory we had just been experiencing. We were jerked back from the wonderful past to the present menacing time of the Islamic Republic of Iran. Our current conversation was actually a very dangerous criminal offense. I purposely defused the situation by inquiring of the Rabbi, "Where are the tombs of Esther and Mordecai?" He turned to one end of the synagogue and pointed to a low small portal.

The Rabbi crouched down and led us through the opening into a small room with the atmosphere of an old museum. Inside the cramped room were two wooden daises and up on each sat a sarcophagus. At the end of each of the dais were plaques with names of Mordecai and Esther. We touched the sarcophagi, spent a few minutes and then we left the room. Though it was fascinating, the tomb room was really a step down in inspiration from the discovery of the synagogue.

The unexpected find of a synagogue at Esther and Mordecai's tomb in Hamadan set the stage for the dramatic events about to unfold.

We had started our pilgrimage and we were on God's road. God was starting to show up unexpectedly at turns in the path. There is an amazing sense of discovery when you walk in these great places of history. My mind always thinks about the countless generations of people who have lived out their lives and purposes in the place. I also think of the artifacts waiting to be discovered. It would be intriguing to see the results of Carbon 14 dating on the bodies interred in the tombs of Mordecai and Esther. Linda and I have found so many interesting places in the world that need to be studied further. There are a host of fascinating places that have not yet been investigated by historians, archaeologists, and other scientists. It has been my privilege to visit many such locations and I can tell you that on the road of God it is a tremendously enriching experience.

That day after we left the synagogue, the Iranian translator and I had an intensive conversation. He was astounded by the events of the day and the history he had witnessed.

I explained to him that a full account of Queen Esther and her uncle Mordecai could be found in my Holy Book. He responded with keen interest. I knew I was treading in dangerous waters but I took a plunge. "Would you like to read it with me?" I invited. The next morning he came to my room and we read the Book of Esther together. We had a long and for me, tense conversation. Every time I would see the opportunity I would take another plunge into the Biblical truths that I knew were forbidden for him by the Islamic Republic of Iran. I met privately with the guide because I couldn't chance the driver knowing of our conversation and I didn't want my wife implicated in case of any adverse consequences. His interest and receptivity caused me to understand that there was a divine destiny in store for him.

Many Oriental cultures perceive a series of fortuitous events that synchronize with unusual timing to be signs of destiny. In the Bible book named for her, Queen Esther is promoted in a series of unlikely events from a concubine status to that of Queen. Her promotion coincides with an intended mass extermination of Jews. She, being a Jewess, is asked by her uncle Mordecai to use her influence and speak to King Xerxes. She is reluctant, as she knows she could be killed. Mordecai encourages her with the statement; "Maybe you have been brought into the kingdom for such a time as this." He is telling her that the series of fortuitous events that have led to her coronation, and that coincide with the predicament of her people, are signs of a destiny. Her very purpose in life is to set her people free in a time of extreme danger. Mordecai explains this as the true reason for everything that has happened in Esther's life.

The scenario we had just experienced was astounding. There we were in Persia at the site of Queen Esther's tomb, reading the story of Queen Esther to a Moslem man in order to bring God's deliverance to him. Our emotions were ambivalent. We were happy for the interest of the Moslem man in the message of God, but we had both stepped into potentially very dangerous ground.

Our entire civilization is being radically altered by Divine plan. New world coalitions are being formed. Former enemies within the Moslem world are now allying under the banner of Islam. Previous foes like Russia and the United States are mustering to the call of a war against terrorism. World scenarios that would have seemed totally impossible just a decade ago are now a reality. One might ask what is the purpose of all this? Simply put, the scenarios that have developed are forcing nations to commit to decisions that they would never have attempted before.

For decades there has been an unholy alliance between the United States and Islamic dictatorships for the sake of oil money. It would take an incredible crisis for the United States to betray this treacherous covenant. All the reader has to do is research the past history of political and human rights violations of Islamic dictatorships, such as Saudi Arabia, to see the wickedness. Yet the democracies of the west have always remained silent. The relationship has been a disgusting one. The only way to breach the contract is for the political powers compromised by oil and money to be forced to back out of their otherwise inviolable agreements. The only way any co-operating party would withdraw would be for the sake of self-preservation. The Arab oil cartels and the power of the petro-dollar are being toppled in order that God's Divine purposes might be performed. As they fall, the repression that prevented God's message will be destroyed. In some countries like Saudi Arabia, people will be free for the first time in almost fourteen hundred years!

We drove alongside the Behistun inscription, stopped and took pictures totally in awe of the effect of that mountain. Then we continued to the city of Kermanshah, the cultural center of western Iran. Kermanshah is the interesting site of ruins and rock carvings left from the Sasanid rulers who were conquered by Arab invaders forcing them into the Islamic religion. Our next destination from Kermanshah was to be Dezful.

On the road to Dezful we were rewarded with a feast for the eyes. A large caravan of Khuzi was moving across the countryside. The Khuzi are descendants of the original inhabitants of the region. They dress and look like gypsies and live a migratory life. The women are excluded from Islamic regulations and wear very colorful outfits. It was entertaining to watch these kaleidoscopic people on horseback and wagon accompanied by their camp dogs journeying through the Zagros Mountains.

Dezful is a forlorn place and the accommodations were absolutely horrible. So bad in fact, that we took one look at our room and decided not to stay, but to drive on. When my guide informed the inn manager we were canceling our stay he responded by being very hostile and threatened to call the police. The absurdity of calling the police for a room cancellation made our guide argue even more intensely. I finally got tired and told the guide, "Just give him the money!" I was glad to leave dismal Dezful and be on our way. We drove on to Ahwaz and planned to double back to the area near Dezful and visit the largest ziggurat ever found known as Choqzanbil.

Ziggurats were pyramidal, stepped towers built as religious structures by the Chaldeans, Babylonians, and Elamites. The tower of Babel was most probably a ziggurat in Babylon named Etemenaki, whose location has been identified by archaeologists. Oil prospectors of the Anglo-Iranian Oil Company discovered the ziggurat called Choqzanbil south of Dezful from the air in 1935. I have always wanted to see the archaeological ruins of Babylon so I could not afford to miss Choqzanbil, which is representative of the same architecture out in the arid countryside of Iraq.

We drove on to Ahwaz and the hotel lay alongside the Karun River. When we got out of our car and walked towards the hotel a woman dressed in a black chador walked up to us and tried to engage us in a conversation. Her unsolicited questions were very strange in nature. A cloud of suspicion overshadowed me as she probed trying to bait us into making an anti-Islamic remark. Brusquely grabbing Linda's arm I walked off and into the sanctuary of the hotel lobby. Our guide came over and spoke in a whisper, "Strange things are happening; I think we are being followed." Putting my trust in the protecting hand of God, I did my best to set aside the thoughts of paranoia.

A welcome relief was that our guide now seemed really on our side. He was very intelligent and absorbed the Bible studies we had each day.

There are large segments of the Iranian population that are intellectual and free spirited. They are reminiscent of the "free thinkers" of our U.S. college campuses in the '60s and '70s. My discussions with our guide ran the gamut from current events to the Ayatollah Khoumeini. I began to use American English puns on him and the driver with a straight face. Sometimes I would tell them, "I Ayatollah you so!" A play on the words, "I told you so." I would say this pun with an absolutely serious look. They would look at me and then at each other with a quizzical expression every time.

Early the next morning we took off for the ziggurat. We arrived at the Choqzanbil ziggurat about mid-morning and it was already very hot. The sun blazed down on the desiccated terrain providing a living model on how the Elamites sun dried their bricks to build the towers and buildings. Our Payan automobile came to a stop on the dirt road directly in front of the massive remains. Linda and I got out excitedly and stood in front of the marvelous spectacle from a bygone era. We stood in awe at the marvel and antiquity of what remained of the tower. The Choqzanbil ziggurat is three hundred thirty-five feet square and eighty feet high and stands at less than half its estimated original height.

As we stood at the entrance by the dirt road, a large open-air bus drove up. What came out of it caused the gravest look of consternation to come over our guide's face. About twenty-five Iranian Revolutionary Guards filed out and headed straight towards us. The fact of who they were was immediately obvious by the bright yellow scarves they proudly wore as badges of their Islamic militancy.

The Iranian Revolutionary Guard was to the Ayatollah Khoumeini and the Islamic Revolution what the S.S. was to Adolph Hitler and the German Nazi Party. Intense devotion to the will of the Ayatollah Khoumeini, cemented with Islamic fanaticism, built a wall around Iran in an attempt at isolating it from the West and its ideas. The Revolutionary Guard made sure the people of Iran complied with rigid Islamic beliefs and obeyed the alleged voice of God speaking through the political and religious leader Khoumeini. Their methods of enforcement were exactly like that of the German S.S. Fear, murder, torture, propaganda, false accusation, and every known form of malicious oppression. The Ayatollah Khoumeini titled America "The Great Satan" and doing so made their politics religious and holy. This idea of Satanic America especially fueled the rabid anti-American sentiment of the Revolutionary Guards.

As the guards ominously surrounded Linda and I, I was surprised that some of them were very young. The obvious leader of the group stood directly in front of me.

My guide, standing at a distance, began to pace uncontrollably back-and-forth. He would look down at the ground and then he would nervously glance at our scene.

My eyes met the stare of the chief Revolutionary Guard. We seemed two men standing close in distance, but in reality we stood in totally different worlds. Our mutual fixed gaze was broken by his question. The question issued forth like a proclamation from his base of authority surrounded by his many men. It was not an interrogative of interest or courtesy, it was a demand. "Where are you from?" I took my time in answering, never breaking my eyes away from his. The lapse of time added to the drama of the moment.

We were players on a stage that had been set long before our births. An eternal audience watched on from history anticipating my reply. " I am from the United States of America," I pronounced loudly and distinctly. I spoke as an orator at a podium knowing the weight and responsibility of his words.

Now it was his turn and the drama depended on his retort. He would decide where our performance would take us both. He took his time, not breaking eye contact either. His Guards all looked to him, he would decide their course of action. In their world, politics and Islam united. He was making a religious ruling as what to do with these citizens from Satan's domain.

The sacred edict came forth to our favor; "Welcome to Iran" was his fiat.

The decree was sealed as he extended his hand to me in salutation. All of the Revolutionary Guards took their turn ceremoniously shaking my hand. Seemingly out of nowhere, a video camera was produced. It was turned on and focused on us. They asked me with the video rolling, "Tell us what you think of Iran." Mindful of the ziggurat I spoke, "You have a great and glorious history." When they asked Linda the same question, she politely answered, "You have a beautiful country." After that, they left us and began to walk around the area.

Our guide was flabbergasted! "This is a miracle!" he exclaimed. "Do you know who they are?" He was so excited he was almost incoherent.

As we pretended to walk around interested, but warily watching the yellow scarves of the Guard, he ranted on, "They hate Americans and are responsible for the worst actions against people in our nation." He then recounted incidents where they had brutally enforced so called Islamic morality. Our zeal for the ziggurat was somewhat dimmed by our experience. But Linda and I relished being there and experiencing the antiquity. As we left the Choqzanbil ziggurat our guide could not stop talking about it. "When people in America see your pictures it will make you very rich," was his closing thought.

Our journey took us along the Iraqi border and to the city called Shush by the modern Iranians. It is situated next to the ruins of ancient Susa. The ruins are very extensive and dominated by a castle built by the French to protect their archaeological teams. In the 1950's the very gates of Susa were discovered. It was here that the Biblical figure Mordecai prayed and waited for the answer to his request of deliverance for his people. Linda and I felt compelled to pray in the very same spot that Mordecai had prayed. I informed my Iranian guide of my purpose presuming he would stay back at our hotel. However he insisted on following me even though I warned him our prayer could take a long time.

When we got to the ruins of the gates of Susa he sat down nearby on a rock. As we prayed, Linda and I began to intercede fervently in tongues (glossolalia). The guide jumped up "What language is that, is it Greek?" He asked very excitedly! I told him it is a language Jesus gives you when you are full of His Spirit. He watched intently as Linda and I prayed for Iran, Iraq, the USA and our friends around the world. Afterwards we toured the area and ruins.

Finally we went and visited the site of Daniel's tomb and stood by the banks of the Ulai River. How can I explain what it was like? I stood at the fulcrum of history, the place where the visions of the Last Days came to the prophet Daniel.

Leaving Susa that afternoon we drove across the Iranian countryside and headed for Ahwaz.

As we drove away from Susa that afternoon I again quoted to my guide from the book of Esther using the quotation in reference to him. I told him "Maybe you have been brought into the kingdom for such a time as this." He immediately burst into tears! Startled by his emotional outburst I didn't know what to expect next. I asked him what was wrong. His reply came like a bolt out of the blue; it was from the realm of the unexpected.

The guide's voice choked with emotion as he recounted his story to me. "I didn't tell you this earlier because I was afraid. But before you arrived in Iran, one night I fell asleep on my couch in my living room. I woke up in the middle of the night and Jesus was standing there beckoning to me to come to him. I want to come to Him but I am afraid to die!"

The atmosphere in the car was absolutely electric! My guide was of course referring to the death penalty under Shar'ia law given to any Moslem converting to Christianity in Iran. For all of us the moment was indescribably dramatic.

An incredible surge of understanding swept through our hearts. It swept out the fear and paranoia of Islamic Iran. Supernatural succor filled us as our purpose and the Divine confirmation of God's Final Plan was made clear.

Linda and I began to weep with him. I told him to accept Jesus and that Jesus would take care of him. Divine revelation had shown me that there was to be a supernatural harvest of souls from the Moslem world and that the veil of Islam was to be destroyed.

We had risked so much danger to go to Iran. We knew and felt a supernatural vindication by the appearance of Jesus Christ to this Moslem man. In fact if Jesus Christ had not appeared to that Moslem man we would have probably lost our lives in Iran for telling people about the good news of Jesus Christ.

Six months after our visit a team of American businessman seeking new markets were viciously attacked in their bus. They were saved only at the last minute! Imagine! Theirs was only a business visit that had nothing to do with Jesus Christ.

Today in the ancient land of Persia the man that was my guide is serving the God of the Bible. Jesus Christ appearing to that man not only saved our lives but it was a divine attestation of what He showed us would be happening in the culmination of history.

Those events in Iran were just the beginning of what is now taking place around the world. The recent events of September 11, 2001 and afterwards are an acceleration in the timetable of events.

The veil of Islam is being destroyed and God is setting His hand again on Egypt, Sudan, Saudi Arabia, Iran, Iraq, Syria and the entire Islamic world.

Surrounded by Iranian Revolutionary Guard on the Iraqi Border in Iran

Chapter 3
The Veil of Islam:
The Rational and Historical Proof of the Deception of Islam.

"Half a truth is often a great lie."
Benjamin Franklin

"If we objectively study the historical record we see that Islam is a deception based on half-truths."
Larry Garza

The Veil of Islam is about to be torn. It is about to be destroyed. I do not speak this in an evil or malicious way towards the people of the religion. I love the people of the Islamic culture. I am not speaking derogatorily about the adherents of Islam, because I love the people of Islam.

When it comes to hospitality, Moslems have it and practice it. They truly honor the guest and the pilgrim. Among the Ismaili Moslems of the regions of Northwest Pakistan the spoken word is as good as any contract. You don't need a written contract with those people, their word is sure. I love the people, music, and food of Islamic culture. Their cities are my favorite places in the world. I'd rather be in Istanbul than Paris. I love Cairo, Peshawar, Bishkek, and Damascus more than Amsterdam, Dublin, Moscow, or London.

Physical destruction is not what I am alluding to even though some violent events will occur as they are liberated from their deception.

The destruction I refer to is the removal of the veil of deception that is over them. Their deception is really the delusion of the founder Mohammed. This delusion was claimed as a revelation from an angel who appeared to Mohammed in a cave. The intent of this chapter is to demonstrate to you that even if you don't believe in God you can see the false purposes of the religion of Mohammed. There are some virtues practiced by Islam such as prayer and giving to the poor. There are some great evils that are an essential part of their religion; war and the violent repression of dissent are just two. Ask yourself this very important question. Why is there only one Islamic Democracy in the entire globe?

Judeo-Christian civilization led to the idea and practice of Democracy and to the idea of human rights. Democracy and human rights are simply incompatible with the theology of Islam.

The visionary Isaiah by divine utterance said this, "And in this mountain shall the Lord of hosts make unto all people a feast of fat things, a feast of wines on the lees, of fat things full of marrow, of wines on the lees well refined. "And he will destroy in this mountain the face of the covering cast over all the people, and the veil that is spread over all the nations".

There is a veil that covers large segments of mankind and the globe. And the origin of this veil is the original transgression of our progenitor, Adam. Now, God has chosen at various times in history to lift the veil. Divine revelation has flowed very specifically in certain peoples, cultures, and places. From these specific locations, the knowledge of God has spread to others. Some people construe this idea as indicative of an arbitrary or prejudicial God. They deduce that anyone who claims that there is only one way to God must be very superstitious and ignorant. They defend the idea that God reveals himself to all people at all times. They are Pantheists; God is in every tree, mountain, and lake.

There is a school of thought that assumes that there are many paths to God. To think that every religion has revealed the true God is to think that every culture has made the great inventions and discoveries at the same time. Some cultures have produced very little for the world at large.

In non-spiritual discussions we accept the fact that ingenuity and creativity have come to us from very specific localities and societies. The Phoenicians gave us the first alphabet; the Greeks gave us philosophy; and the Romans, law and engineering. Some people don't want to accept the fact that the Semites of Israel, the descendants of Abraham, Isaac, and Jacob, gave us the knowledge of God. To justify their erroneous idea of universal revelation they would rather worship a totally bizarre and false idea than the truth.

If we perceive the purpose of history with its many details then we understand that it is "His story", God's story. His story is a celestial drama unfolding on earth that is continuously marching towards its climax. Every generation must experience a performance. All events feed the story line and exist for the purpose of bringing mankind to the eternal finale. Nothing is arbitrary as it only is helping to produce the show. "All the world is a stage and the people but players," said the Bard of Avon. We as players in the drama would interpret the performance from our role but the author, who is God, has a purpose.

All the major religions and their civilizations started with one man and a clan. Whether you call it the clan, disciples, family, or followers, they spread the man's beliefs. All the clans that thrived developed cultures and civilizations. Some clans grew powerful for a time but then disappeared. Four main clans populate the world today and their interaction constitutes the modern world drama.

Today only one clan/civilization controls the globe, Judeo-Christian America.

Two clans called Buddhists and Hindus started in India. Another, Judaism began in Mesopotamia but developed in Israel with a short time of stay in Egypt. Fourthly, Islam began in Saudi Arabia, and its adherents are called Moslems. The civilization of Christianity began as a sect of Judaism in Israel but evolved separately and internationally in the general area of the Mediterranean. By the virtue of its missionary efforts it converted entire nations and ethnic groups.

Islam was the last major clan to develop and is Arabic in origin and culture with ideas borrowed from Christianity and Judaism. In true chronological order of beginning, these civilizations are Hinduism, Buddhism, Judaism, Christianity, and Islam. *While I understand that Hinduism and Buddhism populate large sections of the globe, the purpose of this book is the understanding of Islam's current place.* The Jews have an old, written and accurate record of their history and kept accurate genealogies for a long time. It would be ridiculous to doubt them in their history or for a more recent clan to try to revise their history. Any errors in their written history are what scholars call "scribal". Scribal errors are small grammatical or textual mistakes incurred by the recopying of their scriptures. Christianity is a sect of Judaism that claims the Jewish Messiah did come as Jesus. Judaism and Christianity both trace their beginnings to Abraham and Isaac. Their split is that the Jews never accepted Jesus as the Messiah. The Christians then developed an addition to the original Jewish scriptures called the New Covenant or New Testament.

Islam claims Abraham as their father also, although they came on the scene six hundred years after the Christians, they trace God's purpose to the half brother of Isaac, Ishmael. All their revelation comes from one man, Mohammed. In the Moslem religion, Mohammed is the only one who spoke for God in their sacred writing, the Quran.

Unlike the Moslems, however, the Christians totally accept the Jewish scriptures as accurate and divinely inspired. The sacred writings of the Old and New Testaments are an amazing collection. They were written over a period of sixteen hundred years and by thirty-nine authors. I read them for the first time when I was thirty years old. Their continuity of idea is mind-boggling. Gather thirty-nine people from very diverse backgrounds. Round up shepherds, politicians, fisherman, and IRS men! Ask them to write essays on one topic and see what you get! These are exactly the careers of some of the men who wrote the texts of the Judeo-Christian scriptures. To experience such cohesiveness and unity out of such diversity is amazing. My thirst for truth had led me to read many books before this time. No other books in history have the unity of witness and development of logic found in the holy texts of the Christians and Jews.

The key element in Christianity and Judaism is the faith and genealogy of Abraham, Isaac, and Jacob. Their genealogy is essential in every way. Jesus Christ is a direct descendant of Abraham, Isaac, and Jacob, and His genealogy is proof of His mission.

Abraham's understanding and application of "Faith in God" is an absolute doctrine in the understanding of the mission, purpose, and accomplishment of Jesus Christ.

The obvious historical deception of Islam becomes very easy to see when one logically examines some historical facts. The written historical record, preserved by Jews and Christians, was existent for about two thousand years when Mohammed appeared on the historical scene.

Mohammed had the audacity to say that the essential Abraham, Isaac, and Jacob genealogy they present to express God's purposes in history is wrong!

Mohammed claims divine inspiration and thereby contradicts a two thousand year logical presentation of truth. According to Mohammed, the true genealogy of God's purpose is Abraham, then Ishmael and his descendants. Mohammed is of course the only witness of his claim!

The entire Quran is what God spoke to him and is in total discord with the historical witness of the two thousand year record attested to by thirty-nine other men! Yet Mohammed borrows truths from the Judeo-Christian record and mixes them with lies that violate the original assertions of the writers.

For example, according to Mohammed, Jesus was a prophet like Moses. He went to the cross but didn't die on the cross. Mohammed asserts that Abraham tried to sacrifice Ishmael, not Isaac.

He makes Jerusalem a holy place of his religion because he dreamt he ascended into heaven from Mount Zion. Love the Islamic people as I do, there is no logical development to this belief system.

Mohammed orders his followers to bow down and pray towards Jerusalem, and then after almost being killed in battle with Jews, he changes the direction of prayer to Mecca!

There are many more such arbitrary shifts away from the unity and logic of the Judeo-Christian record. Quite simply put, he either purposely lied or was delusional. Mohammed was a violent man who instigated war. It was his legacy of violence that made possible the control of people and areas. All the major Moslem countries of Northern Africa, the Middle East, Near East, and Central Asia converted to Islam as a result of military aggression, not missionary endeavor. Moslems first attacked the major Christian nations and civilization. After every conquest they have always sought to violently repress any dissent, even from within.

The practice of Islam is violence, war and terror. Islam has no logical or historical unity with Judeo-Christian thinking. It is a total deviation.

If we objectively study the historical record we see that Islam is a deception based on half-truths.

Benjamin Franklin said, "A half-truth is really a big lie!"

Some interesting facts about Islam and Mohammed.

"The Sword is the Key to Heaven and Hell!"
Mohammed

We have to understand some Islamic sources in order to understand the subject of Jihad (Holy War) and whether or not Islam condones this practice. Mohammed is the founder of the Islamic religion and, as in any socio-political movement; the life of the founder is a statement of the vision and provides principles of conduct.

According to Encyclopedia Britannica, there are 3 basic sources for Islamic doctrine and its formulation.

1.The Quran
(Koo-ran) A collection of sayings Mohammed claimed was given to him by divine revelation. This is their Holy Book. In Islamic countries any criticism of the Quran, Mohammed, or any physical damage done to this book is punishable by death.

2.The Hadith
Record of the traditions or sayings of the Prophet Mohammed, revered and received as a major source of religious law and moral guidance, second only to the authority of the Qur'an, or scripture of Islam. It might be defined as the biography of Mohammed perpetuated by the long memory of his community for their exemplification and obedience. Ref. Encyclopedia Britannica

3. The Sunnah
The normative practice of the community as can be inferred from the Quran and the life of Mohammed. Ref. Encyclopedia Britannica

One must have this very important understanding in order to decide if an activity is orthodox to Islam: A practice can be assumed to be orthodox not only by their Holy Scriptures but from the life of Mohammed as well. This can be seen in some of the Islamic cultural practices, such as violence, assassination, Jihad (Holy War), mistreatment of women, and pedophilia, as in the case of child brides and child prostitution. These are justified as a result of Mohammed's life as recorded in the Hadith.

"Tradition in Islam is thus both content and constraint, Hadith as the biographical ground of law and sunnah as the system of obligation derived from it. In and through Hadith, Mohammed may be said to have shaped and determined from the grave the behavior patterns of the household of Islam by the posthumous leadership his personality exercised," I quote the Britannica Encyclopedia.

I give you proof, from the three Islamic sources of orthodox doctrine, on the violent, terrorist, and pedophilic practices of their founder.

There is a point that must be made. Not all Moslems practice violence and human abuse. The reason being, they are "Culturally Moslem." They were born into Moslem families or in Moslem nations but they do not know or practice the principles of their religion.

Also, there are minority sects that deviate from Islamic orthodoxy, and practice unconditional love, tolerance, equality of women, and mysticism such as the Sufis, Ismailis and the Druze.

Some interesting facts that everyone should know about Mohammed's life.

> 1.) At the age of 52 he declared, "God has given me the mission of the sword... The sword is the key to heaven and hell." *Biography of Mohammed* by Essad Bey, page 177.

> 2.) The ten years he ruled Medina, Arabia, Mohammed conducted seventy-four military campaigns, twenty-four of them personally.
> "Those who are adherents of my faith need not enter into discussions or arguments about the fundaments of the faith, but they must destroy all those who

refuse obedience to the faith of God. Whoever fights for the true faith, whether he lose or win, will receive glorious reward either here or in eternity." Mohammed, as quoted from the Quran, in *Biography of Mohammed* by Essad Bey page 180.

3.) He financed his mission by the felonious act of attacking and robbing camel caravans.

"Here comes a caravan of the Koreish laden with treasure. Approach it and perhaps God will present you with it as booty." Mohammed, Biography of Mohammed by Essad Bey, page 187.

4.) Mohammed married a six year-old girl and sexually consummated the marriage when she was nine years old, and then she remained with him nine years. "Aisha the wife narrated that the Prophet married her when she was six years old for nine years (i.e. till his death)." Volume 7, Book 62, Number 64: Sahih Bukhari [the most venerated and authentic Islamic source]

5.) Mohammed ordered or requested the assassination of many men and women and he condones lies as a means of gaining strategic advantage. Quote from The Sunnah of Bukhari, Volume 5, #369

Narrated Jabir Abdullah: Allah's messenger said "Who is willing to kill Ka`b bin al-Ashraf who has hurt Allah and His apostle?" Thereupon Maslama got up saying, "O Allah's messenger! Would you like that I kill him?" The prophet said, "Yes". Maslama said, "Then allow me to say a (false) thing (i.e. to deceive Ka`b). The prophet said, "You may say it."

Some of Larry's travel routes across Asia

Chapter 4:
The Time of the End:
Apocalyptic Visions and Eschatological Obsessions of Scientists and Great Explorers.

**"The end crowns all,
And that old common
arbitrator, Time,
Will one day end it all"**
                             William Shakepeare

"The End is in-sight!"
                             Larry Garza

"Dad, I had a very unusual dream last night," my fourteen-year old son David said while sitting with me at the breakfast table in January 1998. He continued speaking, " I dreamed we were all going up into the air, going to heaven because Jesus had come back!"

His words resonated powerfully in the air and in our hearts as Linda and I had been obsessed with the Last Days and their study during this time period.

I always try hard to be objective in my research and viewpoint. History has a clear record of those who have mistakenly claimed the end of time was at hand. Frankly, I do not want to be even remotely associated with those types of people who replace clear thought with fanatical emotionalism. During this time I often thought to myself, "Are you getting too preoccupied with this subject?"

Yet, I felt I had received a message clearly derived from the evidence of the predictions given in the Holy Scriptures. There is going to be a final spiritual harvest from the Islamic world.

Jesus Christ will herald the end of time by His return!

To this point Linda and I kept our revelations to ourselves despite their mounting momentum. Still, the understanding began as a trickle and developed into a gushing river of revelation. To hear David speak out from a dream confirming what we had been secretly studying was a shock. He was a normal teenager interested in teenage activities. I had never heard him speak about the last days, why would he dream about it?

A seer named Joel made an interesting prediction. The Apostle Peter repeated the message when the Holy Spirit was poured out *en masse* for the first time in the history of the world. They both said,:

"AND IT SHALL BE IN THE LAST DAYS," God says,
"THAT I WILL POUR FORTH OF MY SPIRIT UPON ALL MANKIND;
AND YOUR SONS AND YOUR DAUGHTERS SHALL PROPHESY,
AND YOUR YOUNG MEN SHALL SEE VISIONS,
AND YOUR OLD MEN SHALL DREAM DREAMS"

Linda and I did not arbitrarily decide that we were going to Iran, we were sent by God.

A turning point occurred in the formation of world events in 1998. I have been saying since that year, we are in the final epoch of history. This last phase shall be characterized by a great historical struggle between the United States of America and Islam. We shall see the rending and destruction of the veil of Islam occur dramatically across the globe. The climax of this contention shall bring with it the end of time. Let me clarify what I mean by this phrase *"the end of time"*.

It sounds sensationalistic at first and many have abused the concept. The "end of time" refers to an apocalyptic final day. On this day there will be divine retribution and recompense. The idea of the Last Day has within it the concept of vindication and judgement. It always identifies a critical period of time during which God personally intervenes in history, directly or indirectly, to accomplish a specific purpose, which fulfills His announced plan for the ages. The concept of the end of time has to be a reality. Otherwise, those who have used the fear of it for their own ends would not have been capable of deceiving others.

I have read books that give account of the many groups that erroneously predicted the date of the Last Day. I recommend one very informative book on this subject, *"The Last Days are Here Again"* by Richard Kyle.

Despite the abuse of the Last Day by false prophets, the drama of human history must have a finale. Think about it! There is a final day for all things in our material reality.

Even the sun has to run out of fuel eventually and there will be a last day for Sol.

There are men who claim to have received knowledge to the events at the end of time, the Last Days. Much of the Bible is given to an expectation of the time of the end. This cataclysmic event is called the "Day of the Lord", the "Last Day", the "Last Days" and simply "That Day". The study of the events of the Last Days is called Eschatology. In Christian thought, the concept is called millenarianism because the Last Days will bring with them a thousand year reign by Jesus Christ.

We would think that speculation about the last days would be the arena dominated by the religious and mystic. Surprisingly you will find that this is not necessarily so. Men who were fixated on the Last Days, or on bringing those Last Days about, were also scientists and explorers.

Christopher Columbus was also entranced by the prophecies of the Bible. I have a copy of his personal journal called the *The Book of the Prophecies.* His life pursuit of a new route to the Far East was energized by the idea that he could hasten the Day of the Lord. Christopher Columbus believed that Jesus Christ had not returned because the gospel had not been taken to all the earth. It was his conviction that Satan had established a stronghold in India preventing the completion of God's final plan. Columbus believed that his discovery of a new sea route would bring about the evangelization of the ultimate parts of the globe. Actually he was quite right, though not correct in every detail. The discovery of America came first and with its development the Gospel message has flourished globally. The British and other European powers also propagated the Gospel as they discovered the world.

Christopher Columbus also was dedicated to the liberation of Jerusalem from the hands of the Moslems. They had recaptured Mount Zion when he was a small boy and he hoped to finance the crusade that would liberate it from those who blasphemed the divinity of Jesus Christ. The journal of Christopher Columbus is full of the biblical verses that prophesy the Day of the Lord.

I, too, have been fascinated with the subject of eschatology. As I did not receive the Message of God until I was thirty, the message of a final day scared me when I first heard of it. Not knowing any better I thought, "I have things I want to do before the Return of the Lord Jesus Christ!" Now I long for that Day!

I have had to study the Day of the Lord extensively, because when I speak on a subject, I like to be accurate and authoritative. In order to understand the scriptures on the end times I have had to study the culture, the history, and the archaeology of the Near East, Iran, and Iraq. In my studies I discovered amazing archeological, and historical information that has only come to light within the last one hundred fifty years that is all pointing to the imminent return of the Lord Jesus. The end is in sight!

The Book of Daniel predicts the rise and fall of world empires and the end of time. This book is astoundingly accurate in its predictions. So accurate that it is the only book of the Bible that the date of writing is disputed by the Britannica Encyclopedia. The Britannica scholars feel that there is no way that the knowledge contained in the Book of Daniel could have been written in the 6th Century B.C. According to them it must have been written in the 2nd Century B.C. after the events described in it had already occurred. The author of the Book of Daniel knew the course of future events!

Daniel knew the future in such detail because his visions came by Divine revelation. In the Book of Daniel, there are four visions and dreams that accurately prophesy in the most amazing detail, the rise and fall of all world civilizations and the events of the Last Days. God chose to reveal from the very beginning of civilization what would happen at the end of time.

Sir Isaac Newton was also dedicated to a life of study on the scriptures concerning the Last Days as described in the Book of Daniel. I quote Sir Isaac Newton, *"The predictions of things to come relate to the state of the church in all ages: and amongst the old Prophets, Daniel is most distinct in order of time, and easiest to be understood: and therefore in those things which relate to the last times he must be made the key to the rest.* Sir Isaac Newton, last paragraph, Ch.1 *Observations Upon the Prophecies of Daniel and the Apocalypse of St. John.*

Sir Isaac Newton was to my thinking, the greatest scientist who has ever lived. The discoveries of his life involved every realm of the physical world, with detailed studies on physics, chemistry, and applied mathematics.

Newton was the chief architect of Calculus and the sciences of Mechanics and Optics. He read the Bible daily and wrote over a million words of notes on it. Bible study was a life work for him extending from the age of twelve to eighty-five. So detailed was his study that Sir Newton believed he knew the identity of the last horn of the Beast and the time of his reign. Newton's premise was that the prophecies of the scripture were provided so that, as they were fulfilled, they showed that the world was ruled by the Providence of God.

When reading, *Observations Upon the Prophecies of Daniel and the Apocalypse of St. John,* you will find an introduction by Dr. Arthur

B. Robinson, the man responsible for the reprint. He notes that the Last Judgment can be calculated from Sir Newton's analysis to occur somewhere between the years 2000 to 2050! Ancient Mesopotamia, located in what is now modern Iraq, is where our civilization began.

When you read Genesis chapter 2, you will find that the River Euphrates, which is in Iraq today, was located in the Garden of Eden. In the Garden of Eden was also found the Hiddekel river. Hiddekel is the Hebrew name for Tigris, the river still found in modern-day Iraq.

It is evident from the book of Genesis that the biblical Garden of Eden must have been located somewhere in southern Iraq. Our modern-day archeologists tell us that the earliest evidence of man's civilization is found in Mesopotamia. Why? That's where the Garden of Eden was located! Mesopotamia means the land of two rivers. The region fed by the Tigris and Euphrates is where men first lived in cities. This area is where social laws and writing were first formulated.

The Great Pyramids in Egypt were built approximately 2,500 B.C., or four thousand five hundred years ago. But, five hundred years before that, men were already writing books in Mesopotamia, modern-day Iraq. Why? Again that's where the Garden of Eden was located.

Paradise was where man first had the knowledge of God. Civilization is man's attempt to regain Paradise lost.

In Paradise, the environment was controlled and posed no danger. Living in hot and humid Houston I am constantly reminded that the aim of civilization and technology is to master the environment.

In Africa, anthropologist Donald Johanson, found a human-like fossil he called "Lucy".

Lucy was what anthropologists call a hominid, a two-footed walking creature very close in physical structure to mankind.Lucy is supposed to be representative of the physical origins of mankind.The problem is, around the skeleton of "Lucy," and others they have since found like her, there are no artifacts. There were no vases, no pottery and no signs of campfires. What makes mankind so extraordinary on the planet is our technological civilization.

No one can argue we are physically related to apes. Ask any child watching the monkeys at the zoo. Lucy and all the other related hominids are honestly just the remains of animals, not men. But, ancient Mesopotamia, which the Bible is constantly alluding to, is where you find the first remains of man's ancient civilizations. This is where scholars still find ancient artifacts with the skeletons they uncover. This location is also where the Book of Daniel took place.

Nebuchadnezzar came to power as the king of Babylon in 605 B.C. Shortly after, he took the children of Jerusalem captive and took them to Babylon. It was to this emperor of the world's first cosmopolitan civilization that God revealed the future in a night-vision, and showed him the rise and fall of all world civilizations. Daniel was called before Nebuchadnezzar to interpret those visions. Then, because of what Daniel learned, he began to receive open visions of what God would do through all of history. Why? God wanted to show that He has been in control from the very beginning. God told Daniel, "Seal this knowledge up, 'til the time of the end, when knowledge shall increase, and people shall run to and fro."

One hundred fifty years ago archeologists found the remains of Nineveh in northern Iraq. The remains of this ancient city, where Jonah preached, are still found there in northern Iraq.

The traditional tomb of Jonah is located there. Anyone willing to risk travel to Saddam's Iraq can see these things for themselves!

An archaeologist by the name Hormuzd Rassam found the library of an ancient Assyrian king known as Ashurbanipal. Ashurbanipal is known as Osnapper in the Bible's book of Ezra, chapter 4. Hormuzd Rassam unearthed the largest library of the ancient world. He retrieved more books from the cuneiform library of Nineveh than exist from the first thousand years of European history.

Meanwhile, another team of archaeologists broke the code of the cuneiform language.

Working in a museum in London was a curator by the name of

George Smith who had learned to read cuneiform. While stacking cuneiform tablets, his eyes fell upon some interesting words. To his amazement, Smith discovered the subject of the tablet was the Flood of Genesis. Unfortunately, he had only half of the tablet. When Smith went public with the information in the 1860's, there was a tremendous clamor throughout all of England. Excited by the historical proof of Noah's flood, The London Daily Telegraph financed Smith's expedition to ancient Assyria, Nineveh, in northern Iraq, to find the other half of the tablet. The statistical odds against such an assignment were so enormous, as to be calculated as impossible, yet, Smith found the other half of the tablet in a record five days!

For the first time in history there was evidence besides the Biblical account, that the <u>Flood really took place</u>.

The following is a direct quote from the Encyclopedia Britannica article on George Smith:

> English Assyriologist who advanced knowledge of the earliest (Sumerian) period of Mesopotamian civilization with his discovery of one of the most important literary works in Akkadian, the Epic of Gilgamesh. Moreover, its description of a flood, strikingly similar to the account in Genesis, had a stunning effect on Smith's generation...

While preparing inscriptions for publication, he was startled to find part of a description of a flood. His report of this discovery prompted The Daily Telegraph of London to sponsor an expedition to find the missing fragment needed to complete the deluge account. In May 1873, on the fifth day of digging at Nineveh, Smith found the fragment. ***His Chaldean Account of Genesis*** (1876) became one of the best-selling books of its time. The finding was nothing short of a miracle, and, I believe it was a sign from God releasing information on His final plan. Before one hundred fifty years ago, this kind of information was considered myth and legend.

Intelligent people really didn't believe the Book of Esther or Daniel, there was no physical proof of Esther, Daniel, or of Noah's Flood.

Why is it that only within the last one hundred fifty years we are learning these things. The answer is in Daniel 12. "Seal this knowledge up 'til the time of the end, when knowledge shall increase and people shall run to and fro throughout all the earth."

The fact that previously unknown evidence vindicating the existence of Biblical cities and narratives has suddenly emerged is a sign from God that the Last Days are here! The knowledge given to Daniel was sealed up for about twenty-four hundred years because it was not time for it to be revealed. At the risk of redundancy, let me point out that in the last one hundred fifty years physical proof of Nineveh, Babylon, and the Flood all emerged from the sands of history where it lay in darkness awaiting its personal equivalent of "That Day".

"The Last Day" is closing in upon us. We are at the culmination of the drama that has been unfolding for several thousand years. Just as there are events that have happened to demonstrate this is so, there are certain events that must yet occur.

God is setting His hand on the Arab world in power, to provide the opportunity for salvation in the Islamic countries. As this is accomplished, prophecies made a very long time ago will be fulfilled.

Linda and I went to Iran because of our fascination with the Last Days. Divinely revealed by God in dreams and visions to King Nebuchnednezzar and the seer Daniel, they saw exactly what would happen in the Last Days at the end of time.

In his dream King Nebuchnednezzar saw an image of a man made of different materials that represented Babylon and the future world empires. When he interpreted King Nebuchnednezzar's dream, Daniel told him, "You continued looking until a stone was cut out without hands, and it struck the statue on its feet of iron and clay, and crushed them. Then the iron, the clay, the bronze, the silver and the gold were crushed all at the same time, and became like chaff from the summer threshing floors; and the wind carried them away so that not a trace of them was found. But the stone that struck the statue became a great mountain and filled the whole earth." In the Last Days, the Kingdom of God will annihilate all opposition. The message of Jesus Christ will penetrate every barrier and overcome all resistance. He is the rock sent from heaven. All empires have been crushed by the Rock. Despite violent resistance, all empires from Rome to Russia have yielded and will yet yield to the Message of Jesus.

The Roman Empire, cruel persecutor of Christians, fell to Christianity in one day in the year 312 A.D. Christianity became the official religion of the Roman Empire after the conversion of its Emperor Constantine. All Roman citizens were then free to follow Jesus Christ. His followers became a world power. The Communist U.S.S.R. rabidly atheistic and extremely violent to Christians fell apart in December 1991. Despite years of enmity with America and decades of cold war, the U.S.A. did not fire one shot to bring down what President Ronald Reagan correctly called "the evil empire". Immediately thousands, and over time, millions in the former U.S.S.R. heard the Message and received Jesus Christ.

All world empires are to be shattered by an army that conducts no physical violence, carries no arms, and liberates their captives! I was made aware of the imminent collapse of the power of Islam in 1998. It began when I realized that there were two identical predictive passages in the scriptures. Yes, there are scriptures in the Old Testament and New Testament that quote each other. But I know of only one occurrence in the sacred texts where two passages are identical but one is not a reference to the other. You have to understand the importance of this to me. I had been studying the passages of the Bible intensively for sixteen years. I had never noticed this! It was a moment of synchronicity of my life with the plans of God. I saw the moment as a very special message to me.

Then I began to really study to find out what was being said by the prophets. It was so important not to attach my interpretation but to use the scriptures themselves to understand the meaning. The understanding began like a trickle then it developed into a roaring river rushing through my spirit and mind. This is the passage from Isaiah chapter 2 and Micah chapter 4.

"Now it will come about that in the last days, The mountain of the house of the Lord will be established as the chief of the mountains, and will be raised above the hills; and all the nations will stream to it, and many peoples will come and say, *"Come, let us go up to the mountain of the Lord, To the house of the God of Jacob; That He may teach us concerning His ways, And that we may walk in His paths. For the law will go forth from Zion, and the word of the Lord from Jerusalem. And He will judge between the nations, and will render decisions for many peoples; and they will hammer their swords into plowshares, and their spears into pruning hooks. Nation will not lift up sword against nation, and never again will they learn war."*

The prophets Isaiah and Micah tell us that in the Last Days or at the end of time, certain events will take place. To understand the passage I needed to know the symbolism of the word "mountain" in the Bible. The mountains of the earth stand for its kingdoms. The trickle of inspiration started there and led to the book of Daniel where it turned into a flood with many tributaries flowing through the books of the prophets. As the understanding began to gel, in prayer I asked God very specifically, "What does the Bible say about the Moslems and what does it predict concerning them?" I received the answer very clearly and actually it is quite logical.

Islam is the religion of the Arabs. To see what the Bible says about Islam you must very clearly extract what it says about the Arabs.

This is not as simple as it sounds, as they are not just known as Arabs in the texts. The various tribes are called by their Paterfamilias, the founding patriarch of the family. I had to extract from the extensive genealogies exactly who were the Arabs. This was the key that opened the door to the prophecies that explain the role of the Moslems in today's world and the predictions concerning them.

In the next chapter I will share both the key and this developmental process with you.

The Biblical story of how the Moslems came to be and what will happen to them is quite fascinating and accurate. This process will help us to understand that we are living in the Biblical context of time.

One of the proofs of the authenticity of the Bible as the Word of God is that it is a relevant book. No other book in the world is even close to being applicable in today's world. In fact we are living within its pages. This is a reality discovered by Isaac Newton, Columbus, and you, too, will share this opinion as you proceed. Amazingly enough, you will find that a long time ago in the Near East and Mesopotamia, "The End" was foretold from the beginning!

The drama that began there is the drama we are playing out and the key players have not changed. Only now the drama is drawing to its conclusion, the finale. We are at the end of time in the Last Days and the Day of the Lord is upon us.

Chapter 5
Genealogies:
How the Jews and Arabs Came to be.

"Accidents will occur in the best regulated families."
'David Copperfield'-Charles Dickens

"My family came to Texas from Spain in 1739. I am the ninth generation of my family born in Starr County, Texas and my eldest son is the tenth generation born in the state of Texas."
Lauro Enrique Garza II,
also known as Larry Garza

Linda and I were traveling across the Islamic terrorist state of Syria. The situation was tense, but we were very excited. We had just been to the Iraqi border hoping to find a way across the Euphrates and into Iraq. People had not been friendly at all in the border city of Dayr Az-Zawr. Sensing a new direction, we turned south along the Euphrates River. We had visited some archaeological sites along the river. Now we were traveling west right through the heart of Syria on the way to some of the most splendid ruins of the Roman and Greek world. The remains of Palmyra, our destination, were famous not only because of the resplendent columns, but because under the rule of the Christian Queen Zenobia, there had been a rebellion against the Roman Empire that almost succeeded.

We had read briefly of the magnificent remains of the city, but we were unfamiliar with the site. The location of the springs of Palmyra was very significant. The springs of water essential to desert travelers were located halfway along the route from the Euphrates to the Mediterranean. In Dayr Az-Zawr, an extraordinary coincidence took place. We were staying in a hotel on the western bank of the Euphrates River. As my wife read her Bible that morning, she sat down at a table by a window that directly overlooked the Euphrates. A gust of wind came through the window, flipping the pages until they stopped at the archaeological supplement of her Thompson chain reference edition. The Thompson chain reference is renown for its wonderful archaeological articles. Her eyes fell on the open page and she saw the word Palmyra! In fact there was an entire article devoted to the place. She had never read the section before that day, and my Bible was a different edition. The article said Palmyra was the location of a famous treasure house and that the city was originally built by King Solomon, being called Tadmor. *"And he built Tadmor in the wilderness and all the storage cities which he had built in Hamath."* 2 Chronicles 8:4 The prospect of visiting such a place of antiquity greatly excited us!

We left Dayr Az-Zawr traveling towards Palmyra. The road we were on was a paved section of what was once the final leg of the Old Silk Road to the Mediterranean. Before being The Old Silk Road, it had been used by the travelers and even the Patriarchs of the ancient world. It was a direct route from the Euphrates River to the water springs of Palmyra.

Excited about our serendipitous find of Solomon's city, we shared our excitement with the Moslem driver. He argued with us about Palmyra as being originally built by Solomon. The Moslems respect Solomon very much, and they call him Suleyman. For some unknown reason, he didn't want to believe us. When we were almost to Palmyra we saw some Arab nomads, called Bedouins, grazing their flocks near the road. The Moslem driver said to me, "I am going to stop and ask these Bedouins what name they use for Palmyra in Arabic, as they have been living here for thousands of years. "I stepped out of the car with him as he approached them. Even though he questioned them in Arabic and they replied likewise, I understood the reply. Over the chorus of his bleating sheep the Bedouin shouted, "Tadmor!"

Abraham was the Paterfamilias, (founding Patriarch) of both the clans of the Judeo-Christians and the Moslems. He was a Mesopotamian and came out of Ur of Chaldee, located in present day Southern Iraq, to follow God's direction and destiny for his life. He journeyed from Ur of Chaldees, following the Euphrates River, to present day Harran, Turkey. This was the normal route one took in the ancient world to travel to present day Israel or Egypt. Water was essential and to go directly west from Babylon or Ur would take you into inhospitable desert. It was easier to go north following the course of the River Euphrates and then descend from there into Israel or Egypt. This was the route taken by Abraham.

There was a very advanced kingdom called Mari on the banks of the Euphrates River about half of the way up its course. Abraham must have stopped there on his way to Harran. I have been there to the ruins of Mari in modern day Syria. Again, Linda and I have been so privileged to retrace the ancient paths and roads of early civilization. We were driving north of Mari almost to the Turkish border alongside the Euphrates when I told Linda and my Moslem guide, "I can feel Abraham's presence here."The guide told me this is a very famous ford of the Euphrates where people have been crossing since time began!I believe Abraham left footprints of faith that are still obvious in the sands of time. Wherever men and women of divine destiny walk they leave a timeless mark. Others are forced to acknowledge it one way or another.

The current affairs of our age bear and reveal the true and false steps of those progenitors who created the people that are its present participants.

According to historical accounts written by Moses about the origins of mankind, Abraham obeyed and set out from Chaldee.

Because of his obedience he received seven major promises that are the cornerstone of the foundation of his clan. He said God swore to him to do the following:

1) I will show you your land.
2) I will make you a great nation.
3) I will endue (bless) you with power for success, longevity, prosperity, and fecundity.
4) Your name shall be great.
5) You shall be a (blessing) source of power for success, longevity, prosperity, and fecundity.
6) I will endue with this power (bless) those who facilitate (bless) you, the one who treats you with (curse) contempt I will consider him (a curse) contemptible.
7) In you all the families of the earth shall have the same power for success, longevity, prosperity, and fecundity (be blessed). Genesis 12:1-3

This was the initial pledge made to him and there were several very important corollaries to it.

1) He would have a son despite being past child producing years. (Fecundity)
2) Kings would come from his lineage. (Success)
3) His descendants would fill the nations of the earth. (Success, Prosperity, and Fecundity)

As Abraham traveled up the River Euphrates and then down into present day Israel and Egypt, he experienced several epiphanies. In these divine manifestations, he grew to understand the greatness of his personal destiny despite serious mistakes. Every time God appeared to Abraham, He would confirm His promises. In one of his epiphanies, Abraham had his name changed. He had been Abram. Sarai his wife's name changed to Sarah. This was a custom of the ancient world among the Mesopotamians, Egyptians, Romans and others. A change in character, position or status brought a change in name. Thus, Octavian became Augustus Caesar, Daniel became Belteshazzar in the court of Nebuchnednezzar, and Joseph was Zaphenath-paneah in the court of Pharoah. Abraham's name changed from "Exalted Father" to "Father of a multitude."

Despite all the divine help and encouragement, Abraham and his wife Sarah began to vacillate concerning the promise of a child. Franz Kafka said, "There are two main human sins from which all the others derive: impatience and indolence." Often the scriptures give us the very moment of those two sins and their effect. Sarai and Abram had no children. So Sarai took her maid, an Egyptian girl named Hagar, and gave her to Abram to be his concubine. "Since the Lord has given me no children," Sarai said, "you may sleep with my servant girl, and her children shall be mine."And Abram agreed. (This took place ten years after Abram had first arrived in the land of Canaan.) So he slept with Hagar, and she conceived; and when she realized she was pregnant, she became very proud and arrogant toward her mistress, Sarai.

Then Sarai said to Abram, "It's all your fault for now this servant girl of mine despises me, though I myself gave her the privilege of being your wife. May the Lord judge you for doing this to me!" "You have my permission to punish the girl as you see fit," Abram replied. So Sarai beat her and she ran away. The Angel of the Lord found her beside a desert spring along the road to Shur. *The Living Bible*, Genesis 16:1-7 The sacred texts of the Judeo-Christian clan never whitewash the stories of the patriarchs. Much like a Shakespearian drama, we are always shown the weakness and failing of the hero. Unlike the Shakespearian drama, God in the scriptures always restores the hero to his destiny because His promise is infallible. The mistake of Abraham and Sarah was truly horrible. They used a servant girl for their desire of a child then threw her out when jealousy came between her and Sarah! The consequences were devastating then and continue to be so now. That sin became a backdrop for a drama that continues to this day and is now consuming the world! In a special theophany, God appeared to the servant girl Hagar. The Angel of the Lord found her beside a desert spring along the road to Shur.

The Angel, "Hagar, Sarai's maid, where have you come from, and where are you going?"

Hagar, "I am running away from my mistress."

The Angel, "Return to your mistress and act as you should, for I will make you into a great nation. Yes, you are pregnant and your baby will be a son, and you are to name him Ishmael ('God hears'), because God has heard your woes. This son of yours will be a wild one—free and untamed as a wild ass! He will be against everyone, and everyone will feel the same toward him. But he will live near the rest of his kin." Genesis 16:7-9 *The Living Bible.*

During the Theophany, God named the child and gave a promise to Hagar, the Egyptian girl, that her son would be a great nation. God swore to her and her son Ishmael just like he did with Abraham! Even more, the character of the child is also foretold!

After these events, God reappears to Abraham repeating His promises including the one of a physical heir from him and Sarah. It is at this time that He changes their names. The concept of redemption here is especially important. Despite their failings, God is bringing about His oath! The contractual agreement between God and man has never been based on man's moral excellence, but on God's oath and His purposes!

This is a great turning point in the history of man's thinking and understanding of God. It is a complete worldview in itself. In fact, this paradigm is to become the measure of truth.

No man can present a system of belief that contradicts this and claim divine inspiration. Any so-called prophet from now throughout eternity who contradicts this idea will be considered false according to the true Judeo-Christian clan. Then Abraham, thinking of Ishmael, brings him up before God. Abraham is told the complete oath, which includes the physical land, is to be given only to the divinely appointed heir, Isaac.

However, he is told Ishmael, though not the inheritor of the land, will receive all the other benefits extended to Abraham.

Then God added, "Regarding Sarai your wife—her name is no longer 'Sarai' but 'Sarah' ('Princess'). And I will bless her and give you a son from her! Yes, I will bless her richly, and make her the mother of nations! Many kings shall be among your posterity."

Then Abraham threw himself down in worship before the Lord, but inside he was laughing in disbelief! "Me, be a father?" he said in amusement. "Me—one hundred years old? And Sarah, to have a baby at ninety?"Abraham said to God, "Yes, do bless Ishmael!"

"No," God replied, "That isn't what I said. *Sarah* shall bear you a son; and you are to name him Isaac ('Laughter'), and I will sign my covenant with him forever, and with his descendants. As for Ishmael, all right, I will bless him also, just as you have asked me to. I will cause him to multiply and become a great nation. Twelve princes shall be among his posterity. But my contract is with Isaac, who will be born to you and Sarah next year at about this time." Genesis 17:15-21, *The Living Bible.*

We are told in the account that Ishmael will produce a great nation of people and that twelve patriarchs shall come from his loins. It is here that we find the first predictions of the Arab and Moslem world take place.

Later on we are told of yet another marriage of Abraham and the Patriarchs that will result. Also recorded at Abraham's funeral are the names of the twelve Arabic Patriarchs from the line of Ishmael.

Now Abraham married again. Keturah was his new wife, and she bore him several children: Zimran, Jokshan, Medan, Midian, Ishbak, Shuah. Jokshan's two sons were Sheba and Dedan. Dedan's sons were Asshurim, Letushim, and Leummim. Midian's sons were Ephah, Epher, Hanoch, Abida, and Eldaah.

Abraham deeded everything he owned to Isaac; however, he gave gifts to the sons of his concubines and sent them off into the east, away from Isaac. Then Abraham died at the ripe old age of one hundred seventy-five. His sons Isaac and Ishmael buried him in the cave of Mach-pelah near Mamre, in the field Abraham had purchased from Ephron the son of Zohar, the Hethite, where Sarah, Abraham's wife, was buried. After Abraham's death, God poured out rich blessings upon Isaac. (Isaac had now moved south to Beer-lahai-roi in the Negeb.)

Here is a list, in the order of their births, of the descendants of Ishmael, who was the son of Abraham and Hagar the Egyptian, Sarah's slave girl: Nebaioth, Kedar, Adbeel, Mibsam, Mishma, Dumah, Massa, Hadad, Tema, Jetur, Naphish, Kedemah. These twelve sons of his became the founders of twelve tribes that bore their names. Ishmael finally died at the age of one hundred thirty-seven, and joined his ancestors. These descendants of Ishmael were scattered across the country from Havilah to Shur (which is a little way to the northeast of the Egyptian border in the direction of Assyria). They were constantly at war with one another. Genesis 25:1-18 *The Living Bible*

We must also discuss a non-Isaac line that developed from Abraham. Jacob had a brother named Esau who was supposed to receive the oath of God concerning the land. However, because of Esau's negligence and Jacob's chicanery, Esau loses the inheritance and Jacob gains it. Esau solidifies his estrangement by marrying women from among the local inhabitants, vexing his parents. He then married into the Ishmael line by marrying his cousin the daughter of Ishmael named Basemath. Thus, another line appears that will produce inhabitants of the Sinai and Arabian peninsulas to be known later on in history as Arabs.

Here is a list of the descendants of Esau (also called Edom): Esau married three local girls from Canaan: Adah (daughter of Elon the Hethite), Oholibamah (daughter of Anah and granddaughter of Zibeon the Hivite), Basemath (his cousin—she was a daughter of Ishmael—the sister of Nebaioth). Genesis 36:1-3 *The Living Bible*

These are the chiefs of the sons of Esau. The sons of Eliphaz, the first-born of Esau, are chief Teman, chief Omar, chief Zepho, chief Kenaz, chief Korah, chief Gatam, chief Amalek. These are the chiefs descended from Eliphaz in the land of Edom; these are the sons of

Adah. And these are the sons of Reuel, Esau's son: chief Nahath, chief Zerah, chief Shammah, and chief Mizzah. These are the chiefs descended from Reuel in the land of Edom; these are the sons of Esau's wife Basemath. Genesis 36:15-17 *The New American Standard Bible*

Let us examine the genealogy of the three non-Isaac lines. We will place them for reference sake under the mother's name. We have here a list of the descendants of Abraham that were not entitled to the Land of Promise. This is very important! The Land of the Promise is only a benefit of the direct line of Abraham and Sarah. All of his children were promised benefits but not all were given the land of the oath. The scriptures say this, "But to the sons of his concubines, Abraham gave gifts while he was still living, and sent them away from his son Isaac eastward, to the land of the east." Genesis 25: 5-6 *The New American Standard Bible*

Also, it is said of Ishmael's children, "And they settled from Havilah to Shur which is east of Egypt as one goes toward Assyria; he settled in defiance of all his relatives." Genesis 25:18 *The New American Standard Bible*

This account tells us that they inhabited the areas to the east of where Isaac lived, the area around Beersheba. Today Beersheba is an excavated site in the border area between Israel and Egypt. If you look at a map you will see that the area is the Sinai and Arabian Peninsulas. So, all the sons of Abraham through Hagar, Keturah, and Basemath settled in the area of the world presently claimed as the nations of Jordan, Egypt, Saudi Arabia, Syria, and Iraq.

The present day Arab people are the descendants of Abraham through Hagar, Keturah, and Basemath. The Jews and the Arabs are cousins! Both fall into the ethnic category of Semites.

In direct contradiction to the claims concerning Islam, we see a written genealogy totally debunking the claims of Mohammed. Imagine his arrogance. Mohammed shows up a thousand years after the written record and claims a genealogy that totally contradicts the writings of Moses!

Put yourself in the place of an Arab. Read the account of Abraham and Hagar. One can see how easily the sin of Abraham towards Hagar and Ishmael would instill a bitterness towards the descendants of Isaac. It is often asked why such hatred exists in the Middle East among Arabs against the United States. The descendants of Isaac, the nation of Israel, receive more foreign aid from the U.S.A. than any other nation. We refuse to recognize the legitimacy of the Muslims false claim to the land of Israel. To the Muslim, we are constantly confirming to them their secondary position to Isaac! If carefully scrutinized we can see that their obsession is not based upon current reason but in the ancient rejection of their physical father!

Their founder Mohammed, rewrote history almost two thousand years after it was established.

The religion of Islam is a rationalization of the Ishmaelite bitterness towards the sons of Isaac.

Islam is a religion of justification of the false pride resulting from the rejection of their father Abraham centuries ago. The basis of the Muslim religion is their claim that Ishmael was the chosen heir. In fact, Mohammed tries to tell us that it was Ishmael, not Isaac that was taken into the Land of Moriah, for sacrifice.

Then Mohammed names Jerusalem a Holy Place for the Arabs! Once we understand the basis for this hate, we can understand the very violent nature of its adherents. Their obsession with Jerusalem becomes visible like the ranting of a family heir who feels they have been cheated in the inheritance. The sudden greed of the brothers and sisters so soon after the death of their parent has never ceased to amaze me. The smallest trinket becomes the motivation for a lifetime feud. See then that the wound of rejection by their Patriarch Abraham has been deepened by lack of support of the most powerful nation in the history of the world, the United States of America. This nation has literally sided with Isaac in our interpretation of the reading of the will! Additionally, salt has been poured into the wound by the fact that every war the Arabs have started against Israel since the inception of that state in 1948 has been lost in a humiliating fashion.

What they do not seem to see is that they have more land and more potential wealth than the sons of Isaac, the Jews! The Arab nations were blessed, too. They just didn't get the little portion of land on the shores of the Mediterranean called Israel. That was for a reason.

God had in mind a spiritual legacy for the world that encompasses all peoples.

The apostle Paul, himself a descendant of Isaac, gave up his physical inheritance for a far greater one! Paul's genius explains the true purpose of God's pledges to Abraham: "<u>Therefore, be sure that it is those who are of faith who are sons of Abraham. And the Scripture, foreseeing that God would justify the Gentiles by faith, preached the gospel beforehand to Abraham, saying, "ALL THE NATIONS SHALL BE BLESSED IN YOU." So then those who are of faith are blessed with Abraham, the believer.</u>" Galatians 3:7-9 New American Standard

Politicians need to realize the potential power of Christianity in the 21st century. It is a creed that transcends nationalism and ethnic politics! For the good of their people, the Moslems need to stop identifying with the sordid soap opera of Hagar and Sarah. Yet, they can't, so long as they adhere to Mohammed's false revision of established history.

Today they are still sidetracked with the false presentation by Mohammed of God's plan for man. Mohammed must be relegated to where he belongs, the mistake pile of history.

To do this requires the greatest of human strength, the ability to admit wrong. Abraham's indiscretion is only a side plot in the story. The true plot is the liberation of all humanity through Jesus Christ. Islam explains God's plan from an ethnic point of view. Christianity explains God's plan from a universal worldview teaching one race of people. No matter where you began, you can "be born again" into a new race of people who have a new spiritual nature. This race is the one entitled to the promises of Abraham from God! Again, God uses the greatness of the genius of the apostle Paul to explain it to us: "<u>For you are all sons of God through faith in Christ Jesus. For all of you who were baptized into Christ have clothed yourselves with</u>

Christ. There is neither Jew nor Greek, there is neither slave nor free man, there is neither male nor female; for you are all one in Christ Jesus. And if you belong to Christ, then you are Abraham's offspring, heirs according to promise." Galatians 3:26-29

When the sacred texts of the Judeo-Christian heritage are taken to their conclusion we find that Abraham and the line of Isaac are not sole beneficiaries of God's promises, but all of humanity! My viewpoint is this: If the Jews want to permanently occupy Jerusalem, I really don't care! I have been there several times. *My inheritance is far greater than that city.*

In fact, it is an understanding of my inheritance that caused me to travel the whole Earth. I have circled the globe on nine separate occasions, traveling from country to country. I have not just traveled to the cosmopolitan cities, but the remote areas as well. I have traversed the continent of Asia by land. I lost count of the times I crossed the Pacific and the Atlantic.

My inheritance is far greater than my ethnic or national origins. God has a solution to the present predicament with all of its convolutions. The Ishmael schism is going to be absorbed back into the Isaac line! To do so will take the breaking of the Arabic pride. Muslims must, as all people, humble themselves in order to obtain their redemption.

The world scenario we are presently in is the instrument of their very deliverance. As long as they were left to their obstinacy, they would perish. During the fall of Islam many of its followers will be forced to face the lies of Mohammed. They will confront the deception if for no other reason than that of personal shame. When the doctrines and practices of Islam are made public, they are found to be very embarrassing to the enlightened mind of modern Arabs.

Who wants a spiritual founder who repeatedly had sex with a nine-year-old girl?

What intelligent person wants to admit that their religious apostle was a murderer and terrorist?

How can you recount the proud history of your religion to your children when they see the image of an airplane smashing into the World Trade Center again and again?

How do you extol the benefits of your civilization for the 21st century when virtually all Islamic Republics are dictatorships?

The deception of Islam has reached its limits. It's a falsehood that must of necessity be exposed, in its very practices. The veil of Islam is being torn and millions will be set free. Just as Medieval Feudalism lost its stranglehold in the Renaissance, the Reformation, and the Industrial Revolution, so Islam will lose its chokehold with the Computer Age, Global Christianity, and Cyberspace.

The global war against terrorism had to happen. Furthermore, not only was the restoration of the Ishmael line predicted by the prophets but the current age of Information and Travel Technology as well. Daniel told us, "In the last days knowledge shall increase and men shall run to and fro throughout the whole Earth." Daniel 12:3 Despite the political hypocrites from our civilization who claimed a love for democracy but overlooked the brutal dictatorships of the petroleum producing nations for the sake of their oil company stocks, we have been forced into a violent confrontation. Since Ishmael was forced out of the house and marched eastward, all of history has been marching towards a climax. The last story line left unresolved in the plot is being addressed. Ishmael will be restored to his family!

Not necessarily as a matter of justice but because it was foretold by the seers of the living God! We will take an amazing look at those predictions forecasting the events and restoration. Because my eyes were opened by revelation, I was privileged to see the predictions rarely understood properly except by a few biblical scholars. God chooses the time, the place, and the people. Like Daniel, we must refuse the accolades of men, and state as he said to Nebuchchadnezzar, "There is a God in heaven that reveals secrets."

The tomb of Cyrus the Great conqueror of Babylon located in Pasargadae, Iran.

Chapter 6
The Heavenly Vision:
My Theophany and Personal Metamorphosis.

"Thine was the prophet's vision, thine the exaltation, the divine insanity of noble minds, that never falters nor abates, But labors and endures and waits, Till all that it foresees it finds, or what it can not find creates."
Henry Wadsworth Longfellow

"I saw the light of the Gospel rising up from the juncture of the South China Sea and the Indian Ocean and it filled the entire continent of Asia."
Larry Garza 1986 A.D.

A figure cloaked in a robe with long hair and beard was walking straight toward me.

I was obviously the purpose of his direction. When He got close enough that I could distinguish His features, I recognized the classic face of Jesus Christ! He advanced steadily towards me, walked right up to me, and into my heart! A hot tear mixed with sorrow and joy rolled out of my eye and down my cheek as I lay flat on my back.

The group I was with was practicing Raja Yoga and we were deep in a meditation sequence that was verbally orchestrated by the instructor. This realization of my past hardness of heart against what was obviously the truth caused me to experience a deep sorrow. Now that I understand things better, I know I was experiencing what is called contrition. It was repentant grief for sin and shortcomings of character. As quickly as the grief and sorrow filled me, it was gone and replaced by a sudden rush of love and peace. It was Good Friday, 1983. I didn't know it but this day was to be a giant turning point of my life. I was at the culmination of an aggressive program of personal renovation. Seven years of intensive research in many fascinating subjects had preceded this day. The year just before this day had been one of intensive weightlifting and exercise. The evening found me at the Yoga Institute of Houston. I had been practicing Yoga for more than a year. My goal was just as spiritual as it was physical. I had learned that Yoga was a very old Sanskrit word meaning "Union" and "To Yoke". My goal was union with God, not just physical control. A watershed was developing in my life, though perhaps I was unaware as to how powerful the deluge was to be.

Until that day I had never really believed in the divinity or historical reality of the Lord Jesus Christ. I had been a skeptic and scoffer since an early age. Streams of spiritual, mental and physical knowledge were coming together to produce a mighty river that would carry me away in a torrent of revelation. There were many events that came to a head to produce that vision of Jesus Christ walking into my heart. The week before I had read the scientific report on the authenticity of the Shroud of Turin written by one of the forty scientists involved in its analysis.

For the first time in my life I had realized that there was historical evidence for the resurrection of Jesus Christ. A synchronous series of events harmonized by the Divine Hand peaked on that most decisive evening. Everything that was necessary for me to believe and to accept what was totally unacceptable had come together.

I had a friend named David Tubbleville who was my workout buddy and attended the Yoga Institute with me. As we got into our car that night I asked him, "Did you feel what happened in there?" His reply was negative! I could not understand how everyone had not been swept up into the glorious presence that had filled the room.

A few days later, a secondary experience sealed my new road. A co-worker by the name of Lionel Jagnanin had recently become a Christian. He knew me well, as Exxon Corporation employed us both. If you ask today, he will tell you that he was afraid of me then because of my antagonism to Christians. We "bumped" into each other as I walked back to my area, after I had parked my car in the employee parking lot. Lionel had just come from a lunchtime Bible study. According to his own account, he was reluctant to speak to me but he felt compelled to do so. Not even bothering with the usual formalities of greetings he brusquely asked me, "Will you pray with me right now to receive Jesus Christ as your Savior?" He was unaware of the recent events of my life! I said, "Yes" and prayed with him on the spot.

Again, peace and love flooded me in a very special way. This time it was as though my very perception of the world around me changed dramatically. That day my very nature changed in a fundamental way.

First of all, I used to curse and blaspheme in the course of normal dialogue. The flow of filth stopped instantaneously! Secondly, I now had a hunger to read the Scriptures. I began to pour over them. Soon after that, Linda and I were driving along the bay near our house, taking our little children to a softball game. She related to me how a church had set up a tent at the entrance to our subdivision. The tent was for the kids of our neighborhood and they provided children's activities during the day. She was concerned because she knew my position against Christianity. They had issued the invitation to accept Jesus Christ as Savior and my three-year old son, Alexander, had prayed to receive Jesus Christ. She wanted to know what I thought about it.

I did not respond in my usual vociferous manner, which shocked her. My pride was making it hard for me to tell her I now believed in the One I had blasphemed. She turned in her seat, looked at me and bluntly asked, "Do you believe that Jesus Christ really was the Son of God?" Fighting back tears, and with a hot throat that wanted to close up on me, I said, "Yes!" To this day she says she almost fell out of the car!

I began a process of assimilating my family into the Christian lifestyle. This required radically revising everything about us. Our friends, our habits, and our finances ...all things...were changed to come into compliance with what the prophets of the sacred texts had said was the acceptable lifestyle. Truly supernatural occurrences became commonplace in our family. My wife and I started studying the scriptures together each morning. At first Linda was not co-operative, as she had come from a Christian family and thought she already knew everything.

One morning as we read together, my wife's countenance suddenly began to glow and she began to weep. "Linda." I asked, "What is the matter?" Linda, filled with emotion, told me "I heard a voice speak to me, go into all the world and preach the Gospel to every creature!"

From that day on my wife was a totally different person. She gladly entered into all the new lifestyle I was implementing for our family. Our growth and productivity as a family accelerated greatly from that point on. Oracles kept coming into our lives. It is not sufficient to simply say that the oracles predicted our personal futures. They did more than that, as they provided direction, guidance, comfort, inspiration and many other necessary conditions for a successful supernatural life.

It was 1984 and we as a family were experiencing a great unfolding of the Christian life. One of the areas of my personal growth was in prayer. A friend by the name of Jimmy Stroud introduced me to a book about the Azusa Street Movement. It was a burst of miraculous Christianity that occurred in Pasadena, California in the early twentieth century that spread around the globe. As I read the book I became fascinated with their devotion to prolonged prayer and the resultant miracles. I felt I should learn to pray as they did. It seemed at the time that if I prayed for five minutes I ran out of subjects and attention span! I began to experiment by rising even before our family study time and praying. I learned so many things and it grew to the point where I was spending an hour in prayer before our family time. At the same time our family study was also increasing in knowledge and productivity. As a family we read all the way through the Old and New Covenants together several times.

One morning as I rose to pray, I had Psalm 2 open before me, and it seemed as if a light from Heaven shone down on a particular verse. I knew that it was a message especially for me. "Only ask it of me, and I will make your inheritance the nations, your possession the ends of the earth." I understood immediately that I would travel all over the world.

Yet even more than that I had a destiny awaiting me that had to do with the nations of the world. Yes, in fact, there was a legacy laid up for me that until that point I had no knowledge of.

I came down the stairs to the family breakfast table very excited. I told my wife and children who were gathered together for breakfast, "Today God has given me the nations as my inheritance!" It was quite a statement for a family that until that time had only known as an international trip an occasional drive into Northern Mexico! I can vividly remember telling my friends at my job of the message I had received. Some did not know what to think. Others were irritated. Some were worried. From that point on I had a great anticipation of what I had been told by oracle and every part of my being yearned for its fulfillment. Just ahead was a very dramatic confirmation of what had been told me, and the dramatic beginning of a whole new life.

Late one night in 1985, I was in my living room studying intensely. I had never read the sacred texts of the Old and New Covenants until the year before. Reading them all and understanding them was quite a task. It was all very new to me and yet I was experiencing such energy. It was not a matter of forced concentration, but it was a labor of joy. When I read the predictions of the seers, some of their words would jump off of the pages and personalize for me. It was as if Isaiah or Jeremiah were speaking directly to me. Every time this would happen my soul would energize and the forces of hope and faith would fill me.

Suddenly, an abrupt change took place in the atmosphere of the room. A presence filled my room and my consciousness also made an amazing transition. I became intensely aware of a message being given to me from a Divine source. God was the author because the instruction was a mandate. It had an authority that I did not have to try to discern; it was as if the communication and authority were one. Experientially, I was to learn that this was the Holy Spirit. The knowledge that I would work for God full time became a fact to me that night. I use the terminology "knowledge" because I heard no voice. It just became a reality in my consciousness. Specific instructions were given and my life was set upon a divinely charted mission. It was told to me that I would first operate in a prophetic capacity, after which I was to function as a special emissary. Great men would be sent to help me with my mission. This was a strange moment. I was being spoken to but I was not hearing speech. Yet, I was in communication with the Holy Spirit. I have the temerity to say the voice was Divine because years have passed and I have been able to accomplish what was told me that night. These accomplishments have not been due to my personal power but because of the power of the Divine authority that spoke to me. It is nothing less than a miracle that I am still alive and well, after all I've done and seen. Excitedly, I ran upstairs and told my wife what had just happened. I told her it had just been revealed to me that I would work fulltime for God. Her reaction was not enthusiastic at all. We were making more money than we had ever made in our lives. She had graduated from being a homemaker to having a very fulfilling career with NASA at the Johnson Space Center. She interrupted my enthusiasm with this reply, "How in the world will we ever be able to do that?" Her number one concern was finances.

In prayer the next day, I told my God, the God of the Bible, "I want to obey You, but I can't if my wife is not with me 100%." Three days later she came out of her prayer time and told me, "Larry, I am with you in whatever you do. I will always follow you."

Immediately a release came over me to follow my mission and

directives. I informed the elders of the Christian community I was a part of, as to what happened. They were cautious for me and probably worried for my family's welfare. Now with the experience of life behind me, I know that they were concerned that I was taken up in the exhilaration of my newly found faith. They didn't want me shipwrecked. I imagine also because the miracles it would take to complete my mission are not commonly seen today, they were doubtful as to my success.

Let me give this advice to the inspired and to divinely directed readers of this book: Only God sees your true potential. Man cannot see your true potential and you can't either.

I like to put it this way; you can be one of three people:
    A)   Who others think you are.
    B)   Who you think you should be.
    C)   Who God knows you are!

The first man sent to me was also a verbal supernatural confirmation of what I asserted had been told to me. Our local community of followers was gathered together, a group of about two to three hundred people. A visitor appeared in our midst and was obviously from a different culture and nation. He was acknowledged by the chief elder and introduced as being from India. After his introduction, the leader inquired of him, "What brought you to our meeting today?" He said, "I could not sleep last night and I kept thinking about this assembly, so I decided I had better come here today." The morning meeting passed and afterwards I met our guest. I found out that he was from India and often traveled to Southeast Asia. In our evening meeting, suddenly, the unexpected happened. The man from India jumped up and motioned to be recognized. The chief elder acknowledged him. He said, "God has a word for this man," indicating me! Our leader replied, "Tell it to him." The short, Asian Indian man began speaking as an oracle to me. His voice boomed and the tone was not his own. He spoke very loudly almost shouting. As he spoke, things only I knew about my past were revealed in demonstration that it was truly an oracle. Only God knew those things and most certainly not this man I had never met before. "Even when you were in your mother's womb attempts were made to stop your destiny!" he exclaimed.

Then his statements went from past events to predictions of my future. This statement resounded through the room and my consciousness. "You will travel around the world and you shall cross the ocean many times." His predictions were long and detailed. It was an intense spiritual and emotional experience. I remember having to leave the meeting and walking around outside thinking intently about what was said. It was a dramatic confirmation of what had been communicated to me by the Holy Spirit.

Really it was a two in one occurrence because the Indian man and I became good friends. He was a man supernaturally sent by God. In fact he was very much a modern day prophet. He had an extraordinary gifting to know things about people only God knew and to foretell personal future events for them. I had never had a friend from Asia before.

As a matter of fact I had never even eaten Indian food in my life! We were totally dissimilar, even physically. Despite our being totally different, amazing things began to happen in our association. I began to experience the prophetic gifting in my life. Very importantly he would give me an opportunity to practice. I would stand beside him when he would speak out oracles. It was often his practice to lay his hand on the heads of people as he spoke. He often would have me take my hand and put it on top of his when he did this. I then began to feel the same Divine inspiration he was under. He was the first of many who were to be put into a supernatural relationship with me. Some of these men have been well known around the world, others have not been famous, but just as great.

Just as it was revealed to me on that fateful night, special men have been sent to help me. Not only here in the United States but in foreign nations of the world. I use the word "help" in its largest sense. From some men, I received spiritual impartations. Other men have "helped" to open doors to me. Some men have been my protectors and guides. Some men have been special benefactors to me. Regardless, they always benefited from our relationship as well.

My Indian friend and I traveled around the United States together. I would pay my expenses and use my generous corporate benefits to get time off.

Then the momentous day came when he invited me to accompany him to Malaysia. I had to actually look on the map to see where the nation was located! The time off was no problem as I had six weeks vacation every year. However, when I was told it would cost me about two thousand dollars I was downcast. I didn't see how I could get that much money just to spend on airfare. I had never spent that much money on an air ticket in my life. My wife and I had always been generous givers but we had always seen ourselves as our source.

We had really stretched our family in every way including doubling our size over night with two more children. God had sent us two little babies that needed a home and we made them our own. Linda and I had experienced the power of God in a decisive evening. I can remember the moment as if it were yesterday. I looked out of our patio sliding glass door and I said to Linda, "I am going no matter what it takes! If I have to pick up cans from the side of the road and sell them or even if I have to sell one of our possessions!"

One morning as I struggled with the situation in my study time before going to work, I had a visitation of the Divine presence. I was told to share with all my extended family what I was doing. Our associations had really grown. We would meet at our home once a week and people of all walks of life who had problems would come. We were able to help a lot of people, many of whom were my fellow employees. When these people heard of my trip they came forward and helped to supply the financial cost of it. One secretary at the oil company where I worked had gone through a terrible divorce. We helped her to reconcile with her husband. She gave her entire week's salary so that I could go to Malaysia. My in-laws were a very touchy situation for me. I had always refused to receive any resources from them as a point of honor. When they heard of what I was doing, they gave me five hundred dollars. The first help I had received in any way from them in twelve years of marriage was to accomplish the will of God.

In May of 1986 I was on my way to Southeast Asia. Now, looking back, I am totally amazed at the way life can take a totally unexpected turn, even more so when we live by the words of the prophets. Every moment we live is potent with power for change. The oracles from the sacred texts are the catalysts that release the true power of the moment.

When we arrived in Kuala Lumpur, Malaysia on May 22, 1986, it was my first time to set foot on the continent of Asia. I was really unprepared for just how exotic it would be. I could not imagine how much Asia would become a part of my everyday life. I was on the threshold of an exciting new beginning that would literally create anew person. Again, the oracles of God had everything to do with it and it didn't take long for them to galvanize into action!

Our very first night in Kuala Lumpur we accompanied the local spiritual leader, a man named Peter Tan, to break the demonic power from an afflicted woman. When that was done successfully then the inspiration of God came on me to speak prophetically to Peter Tan. Revelatory utterances began to flow describing an attack from certain men who were usurping his authority. The oracle went on to describe a situation I knew nothing about and how he should start a new in a different location.

When the message finished, Peter Tan was overjoyed and refreshed. Even though I had known nothing about the situation I had spoken very accurately about it and given direction for the future. When a message comes in such a manner from someone who knows nothing personally it is obviously supernatural and it greatly encourages. I had not even been on the continent of Asia for twenty-four hours when a great door was opened unto me. This Peter Tan turned out to be a very dynamic, intelligent individual who organized the nascent churches of Malaysia into a formidable group. He was always very appreciative of how I had been the messenger that brought him the answer into his crisis. In the future, Peter Tan was a big help to me in every way imaginable.

Then a personal life-changing event of awesome power took place in Malaysia. Truthfully, seventeen years later my life is still abounding with its effect. I was given an option of destiny. The message came by way of a God given vision. During May of 1986 in Kuala Lumpur, Malaysia I received the Heavenly Vision. As I write this I struggle to communicate such a mighty event and not ramble. Yet, I can never finish describing the Heavenly Vision properly in its scope and effect. How do I explain the turning point of life when it was revealed to me what I was born to do? But it was more than merely a personal revelation of my identity. The destiny released great physical energy. It transformed my physical circumstances totally.

My wife and I went from a middle class American life to adventures that encompassed the entire continent of Asia! Let me mention just one of my accomplishments. I have circled the earth on nine separate occasions by airplane going to at least seven countries every time! Each circumnavigation took me to very remote areas of those nations! This is aside from the innumerable times I crossed the Atlantic and Pacific by air. This does not even take into account all the extraordinary places and people that fill my life and thoughts.

I was in prayer in Peter Tan's house in Malaysia on a hot equatorial afternoon when the Heavenly Vision came to me. Suddenly, I saw a map of the Eastern hemisphere of our planet. Asia was in the center with Europe, Africa, and Australia on the periphery. At the juncture of the South China Sea and the Indian Ocean where the nation of Singapore is, I saw a great light going up and covering Asia. Then I saw another vision. There were great jagged mountains shrouded in mist. In one luminous moment I was shown a chapter of history, a wave of revelation, and the divine will of God for my life!

It had been my good fortune no doubt to arrive in Asia at a great historical moment. It was even greater fortune to have my life inextricably linked to Asia from that moment on. If we want it we can have an inheritance from God. I was given mine that day. That day I had a choice whether to take it or leave it. Enthusiastically, I shared what I had seen in prayer with Peter Tan. He, armed with the prophecy given to him by me on my arrival, was planning a new beginning. Together we made what would seem to be some impossible plans. He would quit his present position in an established church and start a new one from scratch. I would return to my home in Texas and quit Exxon Corporation and return to help him in the country of Malaysia. You can imagine the reaction of the different people when I returned. Some thought I was overzealous with my new faith, others thought I had simply gone overboard in believing the Bible. As powerful as is this bit of the story, it is only an account of how I came to start a new life involved with the continent of Asia. To this point, my reader, I have only related to you the very beginning. Seventeen years have passed and I understand the Heavenly Vision more fully now than ever.

Incredible changes have occurred in Asia, changes in every realm. My life and family have totally been changed. I have been so fortunate to know Asia and its people like very few others in the history of the world. The different races have become my family, and the great Asian cities my familiar habitations. I have experienced a supernatural life of great fulfillment in jungles, deserts, mountains, and cities. The most exotic civilizations and religions became familiar to me and rare cuisines became my standard fare.

In 1995 my wife and I traveled across the country of Kyrghystan and crossed over the mountains at thirteen thousand five hundred feet into China. As we drove south in Kyrghyzstan our course took us parallel to the Chinese border. Traveling alongside one mountain range, our Russian guide informed us that there were more than one thousand mountains higher than twenty thousand feet. He said quite proudly, "There are so many above twenty thousand feet they don't even bother to name them!" Not long afterwards, I was flying from Detroit to Tokyo. The route flies across Alaska. I fell asleep shortly after takeoff. The man behind me excitedly beat on my seat to wake me up. I awoke perturbed at his disturbing me. "What's the matter?" I asked. "Look," he said, "Mount McKinley!" I sleepily peered out the window to see the solitary mountain rising only seventeen thousand feet above its base. "So what?" I grumpily said and turned back to sleep.

God's visionaries and prophets still speak today. God's prophetic words still resound across time and space. If you will allow them, they will take you higher than you can ever imagine.

Garza Family in Tashgorgan, China on the Tajikistan, Border

Chapter 7
Where Men and Mountains Meet:
Some of my adventures among the Moslems in the Mountains of Western China and Central Asia in the place called the Back of Beyond.

"Great things are done when men and mountains meet;This is not done by jostling in the street."
William Blake, Gnomic verses

"Look," he said, "Mount McKinley!"
Passenger seated next to Larry Garza flying across Alaska to China.
"So what?"
Larry Garza

WESTERN CHINA 1993

The moment of divine guidance came in the most unusual way. I was in a great financial crisis as a result of my last Mongolian expedition and I was willing to try anything that would help me. This included a new schedule and daily activity. I began to do something I had not done in years. Incredibly, this novel step was for me to go to the local library and check out books of my own personal interest. I was reading for pleasure's sake, something I had not done in years. On the shelves of the League City Library a book entitled *"Mountains of the Middle Kingdom"* by Galen Rowell caught my eye. It had beautiful photographs and accounts of the mountains of China and Tibet being climbed. Included in the accounts were some histories of the region and the first Europeans who went there. My mind contemplated places I had never heard of before.

Like a new land appearing on the horizon for a sailor high in a crow's nest, Western China and Central Asia came into sight. The mountain ranges of Central Asia, The Tian Shan, the Kunlun Shan, the Karakorum, the Pamir, and the Hindu Kush came over my horizon and I sailed right into them. The people and geography of Xinxiang Province and the Taklamakan desert became a new fascination. Looking back, it was actually a revelation, a divine deposit in my spirit. A new decision appeared when I read an account of some of the first westerners and mountaineers allowed into the region of the Tian Shan. This area of far Western China was highly inaccessible to men from our civilization just because of its remoteness and the physical difficulty involved in getting there. Also the wild inhabitants, various Moslem tribes, made it quite a challenge to survive once you did arrive. To make matters worse, when the Communist Chinese took over the region they excluded any foreigners from traveling there. My determination to go there came when I read of the first team of mountaineers to go. They obtained permission in 1980 to climb Mt. Mustagh Ata, known as the Father of Ice Mountain. This mountain lay directly on the Old Silk Road as it traversed the mountain passes on the China/Tajikistan border. The author recounted that after climbing Mustagh Ata, they went to visit the ancient city of Kashgar.

"The city of Kashgar was still officially closed to tourism. Everywhere we walked, throngs of people surrounded us. When an old woman approached us with tears running down her cheeks, we thought that somehow we might have offended the local customs. She clung to Jo's arm while I asked the interpreter to find out her problem. Tears came to his eyes as he gave us her answer, " I am one hundred years old, exactly one hundred. I

have never seen a foreign woman before and I am deeply moved."
Mountains of the Middle Kingdom, **by Galen Rowell**

The idea that there still existed a land so isolated fired my imagination. First it meant that these people were relatively untouched with the oracles of the Holy Scriptures. Many new people were waiting to hear the message. Secondly the adventure of such far-flung mysterious lands was quite alluring. It was also a renewed discovery of the Heavenly Vision. Could this be the second part of the vision I had seen? The apparition of jagged mountains shrouded in mist came back to me. The next time I was in Beijing, China with my first Chinese convert, Dr. Guo Hai, I shared my desire to go to far off Kashgar. He had received the message of the New Covenant from me while studying in the USA and was an adherent of the Faith. He was aghast at my longing to go past the end of the Great Wall. Kashgar was in a direct line one thousand miles past where the Great Wall ended. The end of the Great Wall was the famous Jade Gate in Dunhuang. It was said that only exiles and the foolhardy went outside the Jade gate to enter the barbarian lands. Most Han Chinese are terrified by the prospect of going there.

Chinese culture abounds with stories of the savage people and desert. Dr. Guo implored me not to go out into this desert called the Taklamakan. He was a Doctor of Biochemistry at Beijing University who had many former students spread out all over his country. He offered to send me to his friends in what he thought were the pleasant cities of China. I insisted on going out the Jade Gate and he finally relented by agreeing to help me. Fortuitously, he had former students in Urumuchi, the political capital, and Kashgar, the historical center of the region. Officially, the area past the Jade Gate was known as Xinxiang province. This great area was mostly taken out of an extension of the Gobi Desert of Mongolia, more specifically known to locals as the Taklamakan desert. In the native language, Taklamakan means the "Place Where None Return."

Around the Northern and Southern fringes of this foreboding

desert run two trunks of the Old Silk Road. These two roads connect a series of Oasis cities and towns that have existed for centuries. The terminus is the city of Kashgar, which was in the old days the capital of the Kingdom of Kashgaria. The majority Moslem tribe is known as the Uighur people. There are others, some of which are the Tatars, Mongols, Tajiks, Kryghs, Uzbeks, and Kazaks. The area was annexed by the Militarists of the Chinese Communist Party through a series of treacheries committed on the local tribes. Consequently, there is a great hate of the Han Chinese by the locals of Xinxiang. It was to control and dominate the area that many Hans were sent out by Beijing officials. This is how it came to be that Dr. Guo had former students in Xinxiang.

There is a curious demonstration of the division of loyalty and culture in Xinxiang. Political China, though it qualifies geographically for five time zones, only has one time! The only official time zone of China is Beijing time! In Xinxiang, those loyal to Beijing have their clocks set accordingly, those not loyal, set by the appropriate geographical time. This means that for a Communist party loyalist the sun rises at almost noon on some days of the year! As we made our plans, Dr. Guo insisted we take his daughter Bing as an interpreter and representative of his family. I was hesitant as she only spoke broken English and was obviously a very timid twenty year-old girl. Still, I didn't want to thwart his good intentions, so I agreed to take her and pay her way.

As I made plans to go to Kashgar, my friend Ed Weiss of Bartlett, Illinois shared a book with me on the peoples of the world that were still untouched by the message. Specifically mentioned was the city of Tashgorgan, the city located at the highest elevation in the world. Up in the mountains near Kashgar and on the Afghanistan border, it was mentioned as having no Christian population at all. Sadder still, no one had ever gone there to share the message. I made it my goal to go there while on the journey to Kashgar.

My first venture into Kashgaria began with a flight from Beijing to Urumuchi. We spent a couple of days in Urumuchi greeting Dr. Guo's former students who were now officials in various government positions. Urumuchi is in the extreme Northwest corner of China bordering Kazakstan and Mongolia. We were hosted by local leaders of the Communist Party to whom we showed a film of the life of Jesus Christ in their language. Their response was very polite and cordial. Everywhere we ever went in China as friends of Dr.Guo, we were treated with great cordiality and respect. Since Dr. Guo was a notable member of the "Party," I was never sure if our hosts were truly receiving or if they were acting in deference to the Chinese law of hospitality and respect for their elder, Dr.Guo.

Either way, Dr. Guo was a great key to the country that allowed us to accomplish our mission and gave us the hospitable reception and protection from Communist officials we needed.

The first time I came to China, Dr. Guo took me around to visit various Party officers. Upon meeting them, I would give them papers detailing the message of the New Covenant in Chinese characters. Without fail, they would take them from me with the greatest courtesy!

We flew out of Urumuchi and during the flight we were able to see the incredible panorama of the Tian Shan Mountains rising up out of the Taklamakan desert. Their beauty is indescribable and their name means "Heavenly Mountains" in Chinese.

In no other part of the world are there such a large number of high mountains in such a confined space with four peaks soaring over 26,000 feet and 108 higher than 22,000 feet. Nowhere outside of the polar regions are there longer or more spectacular glaciers.

In Kashgar we were met and hosted by Dr. Gan, another former student of Dr. Guo, who was in charge of the local government Radio and T.V. station. Kashgar is a fantastic city reminiscent of a time warp from a long lost age. Bearded Uighurs with strange ethnic hats in heavy coats with the most unusual oriental physical features ran the streets in donkey carts shouting "Osh"! It had not been that long since any Christian found in Kashgar was put to death.

Dr. Gan hosted us with various officials and received our message quite cordially. However, when he learned of my intent to go to

Tashgorgan on the Afghanistan border he refused, stating it was unsafe. But we refused to be stymied in the pursuit of our adventure. Linda was reading the *Lonely Planet Travel Guide* and she found a reference to a local guide named John Hu. The *Lonely Planet* stated that he had a vehicle that could be rented for the rigorous ascent to Tashgorgan. The road from Kashgar to Tashgorgan is a ride up a steep river canyon that descends from the mountainous juncture of the Afghanistan, China, and Tajikistan borders. The guidebook promised that it would be a spectacular journey. We were able to find John Hu at his place of business, John's Café, a very simple sidewalk eatery. John Hu was an exception to his locality and era. He was representative of that special entrepreneurial class of man that I call a mover and a shaker. He advertised hamburgers on his menu and imported catsup from the East coast of China! As a result he had cornered the market on the trekkers, mountaineers, and adventuresome travelers here in the remote regions of the Earth that missed the food from their civilization. I haggled with him for the price on the rental of his vehicle. The object of our negotiation was an old, but hopefully trustworthy, Toyota Land Cruiser. In the course of our bargaining we grew to like each other. As we settled on the final price he announced that he would drive us to Tashgorgan himself.

The next day we began early and the drive was truly spectacular. As we drove along I asked John Hu if we could play a tape of music recorded by my wife. He agreed and as her beautiful voice floated through the mountain wilderness, I asked him if he had ever heard of Jesus. He said he did not know who Jesus was. I brought out a short essay written in Chinese characters detailing the message. He read for the first time in his life of the good news for mankind. I then asked him if he would pray with me and ask Jesus to save him. He prayed with us and it now felt like we were flying to Tashgorgan. Even though I have traveled the Karakorum Highway several times in both directions, I have never ceased to be fascinated with the trek. Leaving Kashgar by heading south on a Poplar lined road, Moslem tribal people, mostly Uighurs, line the roadsides walking and riding donkey carts. Periodically, the driver brakes hard to allow for the reckless local custom of darting across the road without looking. In the beginning stages of the journey you are constantly very nervous because one never knows when one of the locals will cross the road without even glancing to look for oncoming traffic.

Upon leaving this unpredictable element of danger, the pavement disappears and the auto begins to climb on a gravel road alongside the river gorge that leads to Tashgorgan. Incredible rugged walls of massive rock tower above. Former avalanches and geological turbulence create a visual spectacle. I don't exaggerate when I say turbulence, either. These mountains are still growing and seismic activity is always occurring. The actual road is called the Karakorum Highway, even though calling it a highway is definitely a hyperbole. The Karakorum Highway was built in a joint Chinese-Pakistani project. More than five thousand men lost their lives to the ever-present earthquakes and avalanches. It is possible to be stranded for days and even weeks by landslides of rock that occasionally cover the road.

On another visit, having crossed the border from Pakistan to China and traveling through Tashgorgan, we were confronted by a huge run-off of water from melting snow. The deluge of water had washed away the road and formed boulder strewn rapids gushing over the edge into the canyon below. I was faced with the choice of having to turn around and try to re-enter Pakistan and then drive back hundreds of miles through the mountains or press forward. I still remember the face of my Chinese driver impassively staring at me as I pointed forward. He got out, picked up a small boulder and threw it into the rushing water watching intently to calculate the probability of whether we would be swept into the canyon below. Alexander, my eldest son, was with me and I turned and said to him as the driver got back in, "Hold on son!" What followed was the fiercest and wildest ride I have ever experienced. There were huge rocks under the swirling waters, and as we careened and bottomed out our shocks with loud bangs I thought the tires would burst from the impacts on the various boulders.

Our Chinese driver had calculated correctly as we were not pushed out over the edge of the gorge by the torrent. It was the finest exhibition of driving ability I have ever seen; of course my appreciation for his skill was sharpened by the intensity of being in the front seat! It seemed to me at the time the risk involved was better than days of hard travel through the Karakorum mountains all the way back to Islamabad, Pakistan.

As you continue on the Karakorum Highway towards Tashgorgan you are retracing the same path taken by Marco Polo when he came to China. On the east side of the road is a spectacular site, the two highest mountains of the Kunlun Shan range. They are Kongur, just over 25,000 feet and Muztagh Ata just under 25,000 feet. A beautiful lake is situated at the base of the two mountains. It is an amazing scene to drive by these mountains and to see them so close, that it seems you could walk right up to them. Looks are deceiving, as Kongur was not climbed until 1981. In fact, it was not discovered by the outside world until 1900 and the first climbing attempt was not made until 1956! This tells you just how remote an area this has been.

Upon leaving Muztagh Ata, the road suddenly rises. John Hu told me it was at least fourteen thousand feet high. It was near here that we encountered an amazing site. On one of the grades rising to the top of a crest we came upon one of the local men riding a bicycle! Some people with us were experiencing altitude sickness and here was this Uighur man cycling on a standard black Chinese bicycle! Can you imagine pedaling uphill at about 13,000 or 14,000 feet?

I had prepared to penetrate the ancient citadel of Tashgorgan with the Sacred Scriptures. There was a problem though in that the local language is a dialect of Tajik with its own script and there was no translation of the New Covenant available in it. There was one available using the Cyrillic Alphabet. I am still not sure how all that works, but I purchased plenty of copies. There was, however, an excellent video, the same one I took to Bukhara, available in the Tajik dialect and I purchased some of those to take as well. When we arrived in Tashgorgan we went to inspect the ruins of the stone city. It was a fortress that dated back centuries and was used in the Old Silk Road days.

Anthropologists call the Tajiks living here Homo Alpinus saying they are the last pure race left on Earth. Their remote location and resulting isolation is responsible for them not mixing with the other races of the Earth. These Tajik people are thought to be the mother race of the Europeans. Physically they are very different than the other inhabitants of central Asia. The Islam they practice is also different than that practiced by the other Moslem tribes. This sect is called Ismaili and the Aga Khan leads them. Fortunately, they are not prone to violence nor do they closely follow the teachings of Mohammed.

I had a limited time in which to complete my mission. It was illegal under the Communist Regime of China for me to share the message of the New Covenant with anyone. Also opposing the ministry was the fact that the people were Islamic by religion, tradition and culture in Western China. As we drove into the ancient citadel of Tashgorgan I was intently looking for an opportunity. It came about in a curious way. While we walked about the ruins and then the town, we were constantly followed by a Tajik man. Instead of worrying, I suddenly turned to him and as he spoke some Chinese, I used John Hu to speak to him. I pulled out one of my New Covenant texts written in Cyrillic for the Tajik and I began to speak openly with him as if we were standing in Times Square, not Tashgorgan. I told him I wanted to distribute these books among his people. He then replied to me that he was the director of the local museum and that if we wanted we could put our books and videos there on a table for distribution! All this and we had just met! It was actually very extraordinary. He had been educated by the government and was very curious as to know who were these unusual people visiting his town.

He took us to his very small but interesting museum that featured natural objects from the region. He viewed our books and videos as gifts and reciprocated by giving me a painting. He was a painter and had several pieces in his collection. All the paintings were of exotic subjects and I still have mine of a Tajik woman milking a Yak! The local government museum became a distribution center of the New Covenant books and videos and our mission was successful. We began the hard but enchanting road back to Kashgar.

Kazahkstan and Kyrghyzstan 1995

Linda and I were on our way to Alma Ata, Kazahkstan and we needed a miracle desperately! It was a chilly night and almost midnight in Moscow, Russia. Linda and I were standing outside the Novotel Hotel located near the international airport waiting for the shuttle bus. My mind raced back thinking of how we had come to be there. I had called my travel agent, Nancy Burger, at City Travel and asked her to arrange a flight to Bishkek, Kyrghyzstan. She replied no one was flying there from the U.S., and in fact, the national airport was shut down! She informed us we would have to fly to Moscow, Russia then to Alma Ata, Kazakstan and find an overland route to Kyrghyzstan. I said, "Very well, do it."

Linda and I both felt we had received a Divine oracle to go to Bishkek, Kyrghyzstan. Never mind the fact we didn't know anyone in the nation. Statistics had told us the Kyrghs were 99% Moslem. They needed to know the truth, so we knew we had to go.

Now a great wall of adversity confronted us. We had to land in Alma Ata, Kazakstan, which was a backward Communist state with a Moslem past. It was from Kazakhstan that the terrorists in the movie thriller "Air Force One" had originated. People who spoke English were rare and we had been warned of the very corrupt government and dangerous situation.

So here we were, standing at the shuttle stop waiting not only on our bus, but equally waiting on God to act on our behalf as we prepared to fly into Kazahkstan. A dark skinned man with Asian features joined us and politely stood a short distance away. Even here in Moscow anyone speaking English was rare so we knew we had an ordeal awaiting us at the domestic airport. Linda and I were speaking to one another and the stranger spoke up, "Where are you from?" he inquired in very good English. "We are from Houston, Texas, in the USA," I replied.

Wanting to keep control of the direction of the conversation I quickly responded by asking his name, where he was from, and how it was that he spoke such good English. Truthfully, I was startled as to how he spoke English so well. He courteously replied, "My name is Jose Louis Buenorostro, and I am from Acapulco, Mexico." I was totally astonished by his reply! I had never met a Hispanic from the Americas anywhere in Asia, and that had caused me to presuppose his Indian features and dark skin as Asian in origin. I am a product of a long time Spanish family of South Texas and I speak Spanish fluently. I felt immediate kindred for my fellow member of Hispanic culture. Pleased, I came out of my astonishment with a Spanish reply. "Yo me llamo Lauro Enrique Garza y soy del la frontera de Tejas." He too, was amazed and pleased at my Spanish language. We immediately plunged into conversation about our location and itinerary. He told me he spoke not only English and Spanish, but Russian as well. Not only that but he worked for a British Oil company in Kazahkstan and was on the way to Alma Ata on the very same flight we were on! He told me not to worry, that his Russian would see us through the chaos of the Moscow domestic airport. Jose Louis was invaluable to us during the incredibly chaotic and hectic check-in at the airport. With his help we cleared the red tape of the post-communist officialdom that enforced rigid but supposedly defunct regulations. Gratefully, I invited him into the business class lounge as our guest to refresh ourselves. As we visited I shared my plans to travel on to Bishkek to bring the message of the New Covenant.

As I spoke of religion, it caused him to open up to us and share his amazing story. He was married to a Moslem woman from Yemen and had become a Moslem to marry her!

This was the first Moslem Mexican I had ever met in my life! However, he was not antagonistic towards us but wanted to know who was coming to pick us up and take us to Kazahkstan. He was horrified to find out I knew no one in Alma Ata and had no arrangements. He asked, "What are you going to do?" I told him, "I am a preacher of the Gospel of Jesus Christ, and He will take care of me!" He hung his head when I said this and our conversation changed.

We boarded our Transaero flight to Alma Ata without incident and the plane took off. As soon as the flight had leveled out, Jose Louis got up from his seat and came over to me. Again he asked, "What are you going to do when you arrive in Alma Ata?" Again I replied, "I am a preacher of the Gospel of Jesus Christ and He will take care of me!" It was obvious that he was concerned about our welfare. His face revealed an inner struggle at my replies to his questions of concern. Approximately midway into the flight he came again asking, "Really and truly what are you going to do?" Again, I answered with my profession of faith in the Lord Jesus Christ. This time he continued, "I have a company office and apartment in Alma Ata. Please allow me to put you up for the night when we arrive." He went on to say, "I also have a Russian chauffer and tomorrow I will have him drive you from Kazahkstan to Bishkek, Kyrghyzstan."

God had orchestrated an amazing series of events! A complete stranger was looking after me. Linda and I were no longer arriving in a dangerous foreign city without help or interpreter. What's more, our transportation was provided to Kazakstan by a chance meeting with a Hispanic in Moscow! When we walked into our host's apartment in Alma Ata, Kazahkstan I knew he had to be a Mexican. There was a huge stack of El Paso Taco Shell boxes stacked in the hallway where we entered! We might be in an Islamic Post Soviet dictatorship, but we had tacos if we wanted them.

Mr. Jose Louis Buenorostro was a wonderful man and I thank God for the hospitality and care he showed us. Linda and I have been pilgrims on many occasions, and people with great hearts nudged by God have been a great help to us.

The next morning, after a night of jet lag and fitful sleep, we set off with our Russian driver, Slava, for Bishkek, the capital of Kyrghyzstan. The thrill of seeing a country for the first time is absolutely engrossing! As we drove along a new road in our lives I stole at glance at Linda in the back seat. She had the most curious look as she stared out the window. It was for her, in a sense, a familiar scenario, but still tinged with the usual uncertainties of our exploits.

My wife and I have always been on an adventure. God's ideal life for us is always dormant in the seed of our dreams and past experiences. Some people put them away and spend their lives lived out as Thoreau said, in "quiet desperation." We can all be who we were meant to be.

When we got married, Linda and I got in a car and drove from deep in South Texas to North Carolina. I tried to live a middle class life for ten years and it almost killed me! I mean that literally! When Jesus Christ revealed himself to me, He also revealed my life as it was meant to be. So many people have such a religious idea about Christianity. Properly understood, it really is the actualization of the individual to his true potential. I guess the look on her face was that of wonder as to what the new chapter of life held for us. I love a new road in a new country because it symbolizes a new chapter of life. We arrived in Bishkek, and with the help of our driver, found a pretty bad hotel for fifty dollars a night. It was the best deal in the city, believe it or not, and we were on a limited budget. All the others were three hundred dollars a night or dumps. When we checked in at the desk, I came back out to the sidewalk and handed Slava our driver a clean crisp United States one hundred dollar bill. I pointed to the date one week in the future on a small calendar and then to my watch. I said in my best Russian, "You come back here." I pointed down and stomped on the sidewalk in front of the hotel to be really communicative! He nodded affirmatively and to the international traveler it was clear he understood my Russian. Without any further adieu he drove off down the beautiful tree lined street presumably back to Kazahkstan. The only person we knew in the country had just driven out of sight. Oh well, we'd only known him about eight hours!

I went back up to our hotel room and Linda was unpacking. When we were fairly well settled we sat down facing each other on our twin beds. I looked at her for a brief moment, "It's time to make something happen," I declared! Retrieving special pamphlets from our cases, we walked outside into the gorgeous Bishkek summer.

Kyrgyzstan is one of the great places of natural beauty in the world. The majority of the country is mountainous, but Bishkek lies on the western end of a basin that surrounds the fabulous Lake Issy-Kul.

Issy-Kul was the vacation spot for the former Communist Party officials. Fantastic mountains lie to the south of the city framing it with snow-clad peaks that are constantly catching your sight. A system of glacier-fed canals called "karez" feed the city with alpine fresh water. Many tall trees are found along the sidewalks and long avenues featuring an abundant number of benches and footpaths.

Round face native Kyrghs mixed with Russians lazily walk along the city streets in defiance of monolithic Communist statuary and monuments towering above.

I chose a place in the downtown area to begin my work. I had written a pamphlet entitled "Can You Change Your Fate?" to disseminate among the people. It was what we had to get started, although it was only available in English. Linda and I stood in the busiest area and passed them out to people. It wasn't long before a very dark skinned man came along and I tried to give him one. He stopped, took a brief glance at the tract and spoke to me in English, "I am a Moslem; I don't want this!" "Oh go ahead and read it," I retorted. Amazingly he did! Then we began to converse and his English was excellent. He explained that he was a language student from the Ferghana valley of Uzbekistan and claimed to be conversant in the five languages of English, Kyrghyz, Uzbek, Russian, and Tajik. His proficiency in English was marvelous, though he spoke in a staccato, machine-like manner. He was obviously mentally calculating his words.

When I speak Spanish many times I think in English and then translate. I speak two languages but both Spanish and English are Latin based. I have always wondered how you translate from Asiatic languages to English, as they are so dissimilar. His opportunity to practice English held us in longer than normal conversation.

A bold idea came to me as were speaking. I knew U.S. Dollars were precious and that as a student he could use the income. I

106

suggested that he translate for me at $5 an hour. It was a risk, but I felt our meeting was divine providence. Taking only enough time to make the necessary calculations in his head he agreed to the arrangement. My newly found Uzbek translator's name was Mashrab. Meeting Jose Louis Buenorostro had been a miraculous event getting me to Kyrgyzstan, but God was obviously orchestrating every detail by providing me with a top-notch translator. As a tribute to Mashrab's ability, he contacted us last year and informed Linda and I that he was working for the United States Embassy in Uzbekistan.

There I was in Kyrghyzstan with a Moslem interpreter speaking to Moslems about Jesus Christ. I thought, "I really need a miracle now!"

The next day I was using him to speak to people in one of the many parks of the city. Mashrab was the first one to respond to his own translation. He became a believer in Jesus Christ. He was also occupied translating my essay "Can You Change Your Fate?" into written Russian.

Later on in Siberia, very educated people informed me that he had done a fantastic job on the translation. Everyday we went out and met people where I would present the oracles of God and Mashrab would interpret. The really "big help" was about to come.

One day Mashrab said to me, "I know where you really need to go." He went on to tell me of an English school operated by a Russian man named Oleg Panushkin. Mashrab informed me that he knew Oleg well and that I could teach a session at the school. I agreed, as it was an excellent vehicle for my purposes. In many areas of the world where English speakers are rare, people who normally would be antagonistic to the message of the Gospel are willing listeners. The reason being is that they get to practice their English and the opportunity to visit with an American is a rare commodity. Mashrab took me to the language school. Oleg Panushkin was a young, and well-mannered man. He spoke English with a thick accent and seemed very pleased to host us. There was a teaching hall with about forty to fifty people, a mix of Russians and Kyrgyhs.

I decided that I should teach on the subject of American Holidays. I knew they would be interested as everywhere in the world people seem to love our celebration of Christmas. However, I taught briefly on all our Holidays. As I wrote them on the board I again saw the Christian heritage we have in the United States: Easter, The Fourth of July, Thanksgiving, and Christmas. I began to elaborate on this theme teaching on American culture, which they loved, and they demonstrated by listening intently. Suddenly, I felt the inspiration of the Holy Spirit flood my soul. Dramatically I drew my wallet out and produced an American Dollar bill holding it high in the air. Every eye was riveted on the currency in my hand. Well aware of their economic troubles I asked, "Do you know why America is the most prosperous nation in the world?" The atmosphere was suspenseful in the room as they waited for the answer. There were students of all ages in the room. I called a young girl forward who had shown an aptitude for English. I held the dollar bill in front of her face, "Please read out loud what it says," I commanded. "In God We Trust," she read slowly and deliberately. I spoke very quickly, "Our nation was founded on the God of the Bible!" The intent of my dramatic explanation was crystal clear. The bankrupt condition of their country and politics needed no further explanation. Oleg Panushkin jumped up and emphatically exclaimed, "You must come back and teach us the knowledge to save our souls!" The class ended in triumph. Oleg and I had a brainstorming session about the future return of Linda and I. He turned out to be an invaluable asset. Next time we were to come, he would arrange for us to rent the largest and most beautiful auditorium in Kyrghyzstan, the Grand Opera Hall. He arranged visas, advertising, radio interviews, and made everything so easy. We had arrived in Kyrghyzstan knowing no one, and when we were to return we would be welcomed as dignitaries. Slava, the Russian driver returned promptly on the date and time I had shown him to pick us up. Driving back to Kazakhstan, Linda and I were quite blissful having seen the mighty hand of God providing for us and opening astounding doors.

Kyrgyzstan 1996

The Soviet red star pinned on his fur hat seemed to dominate our conversation as the huge border guard emphatically pounded his massive fist once on the counter. "Stamp passport, no come back," he snarled! We had already been detained several hours. If we missed our rendezvous it would be very serious. Our Russian guide nervously kept adjusting his coat and his face was very worried. "Are you sure you want to go into the pass, Mr. Larry? What if your Chinese man is not there? You will be caught in no man's land!" said Valentin our Russian guide. "Our man will be there," I spoke back, not taking my eyes off the guard. Looking the Border official straight in the face I demanded, "Stamp passport!" as if a squad of U.S. Marines were with me.

It was 1996 and we were on the Kyrgyzstan side of the infamous Torugurt mountain pass in the skyscraping Tian Shan Mountains of Central Asia. Just ahead was a no man's land of six miles before you entered the Chinese border. Because of a recent war, the two countries did not communicate with one another. If you left the Kyrghyzstan border you could not return. The bigger problem was the capricious Chinese border guards. If travelers did not have a special guide acknowledged by the government waiting for you in the middle of no man's land to escort you into China, the guards would deny entry. It was possible to get stuck there at thirteen thousand five hundred feet in "No Man's Land" between Kyrgyzstan and China.

Communication was extremely difficult out of the capital of Bishkek much less the remote area where we were. The last chance I had to communicate with my trusted Chinese guide was before I had left the United States. I told him to meet me in the middle of the Torugurt Pass on June the 25th when the sun was directly above. Many difficult deadlines had to be met for us to meet in no man's land. We had to cross the entire mountainous country of Kyrghyzstan with all of its uncertainties and he had to meet us with the necessary Chinese documents. The entire time we had no way of communicating our progress or lack of it.

My faith was in God, not in men, and I just as emphatically told the border guard, "Stamp it, I go!" During the tense drama, my team followed instructions and said not a word. I had grilled them with the edict that they should not speak unbelief. Ron Jadus, Daniel Felder, Carter Ware, my daughter Laura, and my wife Linda were all with me.

Eventually the Russian border guard stamped our passports, all the time glancing up at the holder with a look in his eyes that spoke of our seeming foolishness. Getting the passports stamped was a miracle in itself. Our guidebook described how two Americans had recently been turned back after traveling all the way to this remote place. The next miracle we needed was for John Hu, my Chinese friend, to be in the middle of the mountain pass waiting for us. The journey here had been glorious. We started in Kazakstan and were driven to Bishkek. We had rented the Grand Opera Hall built during the Soviet occupation for special meetings. Radio and poster advertised the event. Amazing things took place there. One woman of Russian descent related her story after she came to accept our message. As a child she had been a member of the Communist Pioneers, the Stalinist era Communist Youth Movement. Her grandmother was a devout Christian. She, being indoctrinated to be a good Communist, had intended to turn her in to the government. Fortunately, her parents had dissuaded her. Her grandmother had made an astonishing statement. She recounted that her grandmother scolded her for being a Communist. She quoted her grandmother as saying, "You and the Party think that you are so powerful but the day will come when the Americans will come and rent the Grand Opera Hall and speak freely about Jesus!" We had another incident where several Moslems came to receive our message. They told us Jesus Christ had appeared to one of them in a dream and told them to come!

After our meetings in Bishkek we drove all the way to the

Northeast corner of the country, climbing high into the Tian Shan. Our route took us back around the east and then the south side of Lake Issy-Kul, a body of water that dominates the north central area of the country. It is one of the largest mountain lakes in the world and is famous for its magnificent scenery and unique scientific interest.

Kyrghyzstan is 80% mountain, and is in the very heart of the Asian continent. It is a very, very exotic country. The scenery was absolutely incredible as we entered what is known as the "Rooftop of the World." Drawing close to the Chinese border and the Tian Shan (Heavenly Mountains), we drove for at least sixty miles alongside a mountain range called the Atbasi. This is how we had come to be at the Torugart pass in the very heart of Central Asia. Getting through would take a miracle and we needed John Hu to be waiting for us in the middle of the pass. By the time we had cleared the last outpost before China, we were hours late to our appointment with John Hu. The officer stamped our passports and we packed into the Russian military van we had been using, along with our guide, Valentin.

There was no turning back now! He could only drive us to the middle of what they called "No Mans' Land" and drop us off. As we drove into the pass, the mountain scenery was as dramatic as the moment. No one said a word as we drove slowly, our eyes scouring the road for any sign of John Hu. We came around a corner made by the rock walls, and there was his familiar Toyota Land Cruiser. But John was nowhere in sight. Our Russian driver stopped some distance away as if wary of some ambush. I jumped out and ran towards the empty vehicle. A head appeared over the dashboard calling out to me, "Larry, where have you been?" He was laying down in the back seat, resting. I ran up to him and hugged him warmly, exclaiming, "Oh John, you know, Russian guards!" Everyone quickly transferred his or her items to the Toyota and off we went. The intensity of Torugart passage began to diminish with the prospect of the new territory and our new adventure. No ride in this part of the world is ever dull and after passing Chinese guard stations and customs we again became engrossed in our surroundings.

Behind us on the other side of the pass was Kyrghyzstan and its mountain meadows and ranges. On this side we were constantly descending a river canyon into the Great Taklmakan Desert. We went from a chilling cold to an ever-increasing temperature. A great cloud of red dust was soon billowing behind us as we descended more and more until the windows had to be rolled up and everything inside was covered in an ochreous dirt powder. After dropping thousands of feet in elevation, our drive finally bottomed out into the desert floor outside of Kashgar and we drove into the city. We checked into the Seeman Hotel, which formerly served as the Russian embassy, cleaned our baggage and ourselves. Compared to the Kyrgyzstan wilderness, Kashgar felt like we were back in civilization. It was God who had birthed the desire in my heart of crossing the Tian Shan Mountains from Kyrgyzstan into China through the difficult Torugart border pass.

Linda and I had been able to bring the Message into Kyrghystan and then we had crossed the back way into China. The Message and the messenger become one in God's economy. Our triumph represented God's triumph over formerly hostile borders. For me it was a glorious experience as my studies of history, archaeology, and the Bible melded into one continuum of invaluable personal understanding.

Now that we were in Kashgar, I wanted to launch into a new realm of effectiveness. Knowing the history of the region I felt there must be a remnant of Christians somewhere. In the 12th century, Nestorian Christians had traveled from Xinxiang to the west and visited Jerusalem and Rome. Much later, at the turn of the 20th century, messengers like George Hunter, Mildred Cable, and Francesca French had pioneered the message in Xinxiang province among the Uighurs and others. We woke up the morning after our arrival in Kashgar from Kyrghyzstan, and as was our daily practice, prayed. I told my team that consisted of my wife Linda, my daughter Laura, Carter

Ware, Ron Jadus, and Daniel Felder that we needed to go and make something happen.

We proceeded into the downtown area and walked down the streets looking for an answer to our request made of God. I told the team, "I feel we should cross the street and go in that direction." We did so and walked into a building that had many small shops. Daniel Felder started talking to a woman selling dried fruits as she began asking him questions. I joined into the conversation and she was trying to speak English with great difficulty. We were able to laboriously make out what she was saying. She was Han Chinese and she asked us, "Are you Christians?" I was a bit startled as this was not a normal conversation in China, especially Moslem China. I answered, "Yes."

She then astonishingly pulled a Chinese Bible from under her counter and said, "So am I, and I live by faith in God's Word." Wow! This scenario had never happened to me anywhere in China. I spoke to her and asked her if there was a church in Kashgar. She replied that there was and if I wanted to go there she could take me that afternoon! What a quick and amazing answer to our requests to God! We had been supernaturally guided to her. She offered to take us to the church that afternoon by bus if we wanted. We told her that would be wonderful and that we would return at 4:00 for the journey.

That afternoon, with a tense excitement, we joined her for the bus ride to another section of Kashgar removed from the downtown district. The bus stopped and she led us into a neighborhood of homes and trees. We stopped before a large walled residence. She knocked at the wooden gate that served as the door to the walled enclosure. A Chinese woman appeared and stared at us with a mixture of amazement and elation. We were brought into the courtyard and led to the building, which had several stories. We ascended an outside staircase to the third floor. She led us into a room with many chairs and a large red cross on one wall. Several people came in and joined us including an elderly, partially paralyzed Chinese man.

Our new friend found an unexpected source of English from

within her and translated for everyone. There were formalities exchanged and then we asked each other questions. I asked the leader, the elderly Chinese man who was the founder of this community how he had come to be there. His story was truly amazing! He had been a prisoner of the Japanese in Shanghai during World War Two. It was during his life-threatening imprisonment that he asked God to save him. He became a disciple of Jesus Christ and lived through the war. At the time of his divine rescue he was told by God to go west giving the message until he came to Mecca! The only regret he shared of his life was that, because of the previous political condition of Central Asia, Kashgar was as far west as he had made it.

I was frankly overwhelmed by what I had just heard as I was under the same mandate. Thousands of people during this time period of my life in the early 1990's heard me say I was going overland from Shanghai to Jerusalem with The Message.

Then another miraculous story unfolded. They had been in isolation since 1949 when the only Christians they knew, Swedish people who had operated a hospital in Kashgar, were forced to leave. To give you an idea of their worldview, they asked us to thank the Swedes for them when we returned to the outside! Amazingly, they thought the outside world was one small community and I would obviously know the Swedes! Incredibly the story continued.

Earlier that year, 1996, they had gone to the mountains to pray for forty days, requesting of God to bring them someone from the outside world who believed in the New Covenant. They felt our coming was an answer to a request made of God! We agreed to come back the next day and have a special meeting. Great joy filled us as to what was happening. They called two taxis and sent us back to our hotel where we eagerly anticipated the events to come. At this time there were only about ten adherents of the faith in the New Covenant known to exist among Uighurs of China, despite the fact that their population was over 7,000,000. That night in Kashgar my wife had a dream that a Uighur boy came to her asking for the words of life.

The next day we went back to our new friends and sat together. A

114

Uighur woman was there as well, having been brought by one of the other members of the community. After our general time of visiting together, my wife began to speak to her. She too, had had a dream at the same time my wife did in which she was told to receive The Message.

When Linda asked her if she was ready to believe she said, "I am chosen by God. I must accept!" So my wife prayed with her and she became an adherent of Jesus Christ! She became one of the first believers of the New Covenant from the Uighur Moslems! The Uighur woman asked us after we finished praying with her, "Are you not afraid you will be killed going about this region with the papers you give about the faith?" I replied, "I know God will provide safety for me as the safest place to be is in the will of God!"

To give you an idea of the isolation, remoteness, and difficulty of working in Xinxiang province, let me share a detail with you. Charisma Magazine, a national periodical, had a large article on Xinxiang in the year 2000. They reported there were no churches or Christians in the region still to this day. Charisma was totally unaware of what has been occurring despite the fact that we were there each year from 1995 through 1998.

This episode was one of many miraculous times we spent in Xinxiang. I was very fortunate to be able to retrace Marco Polo's trail across China in 1996. I traveled two thousand, five hundred miles by four-wheel drive from the Afghanistan border to the ancient capital of Xian, China. That was an epic journey filled with supernatural events.

Chapter 8:
Is There Really Only One Way?:
The Paradigm of Western Civilization and its Objectivity.

"The authority of the prophets is divine, and comprehends the sum of religion, reckoning Moses and the Apostles among the Prophets; and if an Angel from Heaven preach any other gospel than what they have delivered let him be accursed."
Quoted from, *Newton's Prophecies of Daniel,* Sir Isaac Newton.

"I was totally convinced Christianity was a religion for the ignorant and superstitious, then at the age of 30 I read the Bible for the first time. I have been studying the scriptures continuously since that day. I have read thousands of books in my life yet it is the only book that can hold my attention to read it over and over!"

Larry Garza

The sacred texts of the Christians and the Jews are the paradigm and foundation of Western Civilization. At one time in my life I thought these sacred texts were irrelevant compilations of superstition. I experienced a turning point in life during my twenties as I was exposed to the ideas of the new 20th century physics. This branch of physics is well known as Quantum Mechanics and it has changed our world forever in good and bad ways.

The discoveries of foundational scientists, men like Max Planck, Verner Heisenberg, Richard Oppenheimer, and Albert Einstein were actually the result of an extreme search for the objective, true reality of our universe. Their lives and discoveries changed the course of my life in a profound way. My life perspective was transformed from that of a materialist to a person open to the spiritual world. It was the sub-atomic physics of the 20th century that opened my mind to the possibility of uncovering spiritual truth. The realization of truth first requires that we be objective with ourselves. If we cannot be impartial towards ourselves the final reality cannot be discerned.

God is the ultimate reality that a liar cannot approach. The seers of the scriptures were not men intent on formulating a religion. Reality became apparent to them and what they perceived obsessed them. This intense love of objectivity and God can be seen in the Scriptures of the Old and New Covenant.

The new physicists of the 20th century gained their perspective by standing on the foundation of thought developed by men like Isaac Newton. Einstein may have given us a new view of the laws of the universe but Newton built the platform that allowed him to stand and look out into that very cosmos. Newton's objectivity discovered the laws that govern everyday life and made today's technological world possible. He gave us a world paradigm, the very pattern by which we perceive reality and life. It is because of his contribution to the understanding of the laws of science that I am so impressed with his obsession with the prophecies of the Bible. His dedication and research produced a commentary on the books of Daniel and Revelation demonstrating their historical fulfillment. As you can see from the opening quotation of this chapter, Newton knew that any source of revelation other than the Bible was cursed. He totally acknowledged the seers, visionaries, and prophets of the Old and New covenant as being completely authoritative. Newton and I agree that anyone not standing on this foundation is not an authority.

How is it possible that a man like Isaac Newton, who formulated the mechanics of the physical world, would accept the Christian scriptures as historically authoritative? There must be an objective perspective he saw that would demonstrate to us their logic and validity.

Every person who is really objective will find that Christianity is not a religion but a revelation of ultimate truth. There are people today who claim objectivity, when really they are reactionaries. These people are liars of the worst sort because they have lied to themselves.

They are reactionaries in that their thoughts are based on a rebellion against truth and fact. Their foundation says that there are many ways to the truth and that everyone is right in choosing their own path. They claim Bible believers are intolerant, but are extremely prejudiced against Christians themselves. It is so obviously simple, if everyone can be right then Adolph Hitler was only following his own revelation!

When we throw away a standard of objective values then we must allow and approve of every conceivable type of behavior.

When speaking about Hinduism, Buddhism, or Islam, reactionaries act as if they are enlightened topics for discussion. In the 1990's people began touting the Dalai Lama, the leader of the Tibetan Buddhists, as some great spiritual being and made him the toast of society functions across the United States. It is part of the Tibetan religion to drink fermented Yak milk from a silver gilded skull of an ancestor! They also make horns from human thighbones for use in their rituals! Their gods are a macabre assortment of vicious bloodthirsty demons.

Tibetan and Nepalese Buddhists practice polyandry as a way of life whereby several brothers share one wife! The children of the mother call all the brothers of the family father!

Bathing is a rare practice in Tibet and Nepal. The truth is Tibetan Buddhism is a barbaric way of thought, and its leader, the Dalai Lama, is also a savage. It is understandable why Tibetan Buddhists haven't contributed anything to the modern world. The same people who tout Tibetan Buddhism as wise counsel routinely consider a Christian with a spiritual experience who uses the nomenclature of "Born Again" as ignorant. I pose the question: Who really is the ignorant one?

Still others extol Hinduism as enlightened. Yet every year hundreds of Hindu mothers, supposedly acting upon special instructions from their gods, throw their firstborn baby into the Ganges River! The same people commending Hinduism denounce Christians who protest the murder of babies in our nation as ignorant! Many states in India with populations in severe famine, legally prohibit the slaughter of a cow for human consumption!

The Christian nations of the world not only feed their own people but also give their surplus to nations such as India.

Flying Singapore Airlines across the Indian Ocean, I read an article in Asiaweek, the Asian counterpart to Newsweek magazine. The editorial, in a gesture of misdirected nationalism, was highly critical of Christian missionaries and the Judeo-Christian influence in India. I wrote the Editor a letter saying if it were not for those missionaries he was criticizing, he would not have deodorant, potable water, or toilet paper! People we know would shudder at the very thought of living in a nation without the benefits of what our Christian society has produced.

The logic behind extolling the benefits of Islamic, Buddhist, or Hindu civilization is ludicrous.

It also would have been just as ridiculous to the great men who established our civilization. Their thought structure was Judeo-Christian. Other than the small degree demonstrated in the nation of Turkey, democracy is unknown in the Moslem world. Turkey is a pro-western country that aligns itself with the west. In most Moslem nations, education for women is rare. In the Moslem centers of the world women are treated as animals. Yet democracy and equal rights are a way of life for women in Christian civilization. Jesus spoke with the adulterous women of His day in order to restore their dignity.

In contrast, Mohammed married a five-year old girl and prescribed wife beating!

I am asking the reactionaries to quit lying to themselves and acknowledge facts.

People from America are not immigrating to the Middle East; it is the Arabs who are coming to America in droves! An Asian Indian, Tibetan, Nepalese, or any other member of a pagan society will do anything to come here to this nation based on Judeo-Christian values.

Now that we have become corrupted from our Judeo-Christian origins, we have people who are extolling the virtues of Islamic, Buddhist, or Hindu societies. They are liars who are willingly deceived and refuse objectivity. We as Americans have to be really stupid to allow an inferior way of life to dominate ours.

It was the Judeo-Christian thought structure that gave us the inventions that improved our society. None of the medical, industrial, or technological innovations we depend on came from Buddhist or Hindu societies. Islam preserved some knowledge from ancient Greece that it encountered in its military expansionism, but has contributed nothing of significant value to the world as we know it.

When studying the Arab/Islamic conquests of the seventh through eighth centuries, you find that they used the already present and educated Judeo-Christian populations to build their cities. The "conquerors" were nomads from the desert with little sense of infrastructure. Islamic culture did contribute a few things. But, if any of these civilizations are compared to the inventions, productivity, or standard of living for the common man experienced in Judeo-Christian civilization, they are revealed as being sorely lacking. There is great prejudice and bias in the world today against Judeo-Christian thinking. This prejudice is rationalized as enlightened thinking but in fact is a denial of the truth. As Newton said, any other gospel brings a curse. The curse comes because people are embracing and living out a lie.

My aim is not to lambaste the deficiencies of non-Christian thinking and life but to bring us to a certain vantage point. The Holy Scriptures are not the subjective ramblings of a Middle Eastern ethnic group called the Jews. They are detailed instructions from God that demonstrate their power in that they accurately predict events. This power was obviously not manifested in men who were intent on achieving a purely personal agenda. The sacred writings are the result of revelations given to men who were first and foremost interested in knowing God. As a result of their objectivity, God rewarded them by letting them know His secrets concerning the future. If God did not author the scriptures, why is it that the issues and peoples that are their focus still consume the world today? At this very moment, the Arabs and the Moslems are creating havoc and bedlam in Afghanistan, Chechnya, Indonesia, India, Israel, Pakistan, the Philippines, and the United States. In each locale they act in open violence. They are also involved in shrouded acts of savagery in many other nations of the world.

Moses tells us in Genesis 16:12 that this was predicted concerning the Arabs in the time of Abraham:
"And he will be a wild donkey of a man, His hand will be against everyone, and everyone's hand will be against him."

The prophecy is more than being fulfilled!

How can we disregard the evidence? No other sacred writings in the world have this accuracy! The Arabs and Islam were birthed out of Abraham's error and their centuries of violence have been an attempt to prove their worthiness. When you live long enough, you will see the same plot in every family, the mistakes of the fathers and the resulting misperceptions of the children. This is very much a result of our original father Adam's mistake. Our global problem today is but the echo of Cain and Abel. Looking at this, it is difficult to realize that the Heavenly Father loves everyone unconditionally to the same degree. Paul spoke out as an oracle in his letter to the Galatians, "There is neither Jew nor Greek, there is neither slave nor free man, there is neither male nor female; for you are all one in Christ Jesus."

God promised to bless the Moslems regardless of anyone's mistake. God's plan works out eventually, despite man's carnal meanderings. His plan is to restore all of His chosen people into one group.

The culmination of the messages of the prophets is the Messiah, Jesus Christ. Moses told us that the Ishmael Moslem group would, "live to the east of all his brothers." This is the area from Egypt to Iran. Much later after Moses the visionary, Isaiah said that God would set His hand in power on that region.

"Then it will happen on that day that the Lord
Will again recover the second time with His hand
The remnant of His people, who will remain,
From Assyria, Egypt, Pathros, Cush, Elam, Shinar, Hamath,
And from the islands of the sea.
And He will lift up a standard for the nations
And assemble the banished ones of Israel,
And will gather the dispersed of Judah
From the four corners of the Earth."
Isaiah 11:11-12.

Careful study will reveal that the places called Assyria, Egypt, Pathros, Cush, Elam, Shinar, and Hamath are that very area of the world. The area just named stretches from the Horn of Africa to Iran. This area is the very stronghold of Islam. How is it possible that millions will be taken into the love of the New Covenant from this dark region? The antagonism and violence seems impossible to overcome. The very drama the whole world has been drawn into with Islamic terrorism is the actual catalyst that will open the region and the hearts of the people.

There are many Moslems who are only culturally involved in their religion. They do not practice it in accordance with its writings. At a time like this I am sure they are very much ashamed to be associated with the brutality and savagery of those claiming to be obedient to the doctrines of Islam. If any are objective, they will see the truth. In fact this applies to the nations of Western Civilization. We need to be objective. People need to quit lying about Islam and the pagan religions. We are involved in a global conflict that has been brewing since the dawn of time. There never has been nor will there ever be a compromise between the truth and the vain delusions of men. A final group of people from the Islamic nations will be brought into the New Covenant and then the end of time will come.

Gate at the very end of the Great Wall of China

John Hu my devoted friend and faithful guide across China.
Marco Polo noted that this site in the White Jade River just North
of Tibet had been the source for hundreds of years of the best
white Jade for the Chinese emperors

The stele erected by the Chinese Emperor in 631 A.D. in tribute to the Nestorian Christian that came from ancient Iraq. The very first messenger was Alopen, his name and other fellow Iraqis are inscribed in the ancient Aramaic language.

Chapter 9:
The Old Silk Road:
High Adventure Down the Old Silk Road in the Taklamakan Desert Across China

"I have not told half of what I saw."
Marco Polo

"To go there is to experience the stark spirituality of the terrain. You might be skeptical until you are there on the dirt track of the Old Silk Road, your headlights piercing the blackness, uninterrupted for hundreds of miles by any artificial light. There you might hear voices or see apparitions yourself!"
Larry Garza

A long plume of dust hung behind me on the gravel desert road as I cranked the gears of the 1986 Toyota Land Cruiser. Working like a man on a machine in a Detroit assembly line, I was on the Old Silk Road in the Taklamakan of China and I had never felt better in my life.

The sun beat down on the anvil of the desert and heated the arid wind that blew through the open window against my face. To me it felt as though the strong hand of destiny was caressing my countenance. Despite the strokes of destiny's affection and seeming good fortune, I did not dare let my concentration drift from the road just ahead. I stared relentlessly through the windshield at the shimmering landscape, ready at any moment to downshift, step on the brakes, and decelerate to change course. The track we were on was one of constantly changing conditions. Rocks, deep sand, and frequent hazards required my constant shifting of the gears.

We had left Kashgar days ago and we were just north of the Kunlun, a mountain range that long provided a wall of rock as a border between China and Tibet. The Kunlun spring thaws produced torrential rivers that swept out of the mountains into the desert, disappearing into the immense sands of the Taklamakan. Their yearly courses left deep crevasses on the terrain that could easily swallow my Toyota Land Cruiser. Because of our rate of speed, they were hard to see and would loom up unexpectedly like a bad mirage. Upon their appearance, I would have to slow down from sixty miles an hour or more to a slow crawl in order to navigate their edges, to find a place to drive down into them and then back up. Some were twenty or thirty feet deep and much wider than their depth!

As soon as I became aware of an impending crevasse, I would downshift and brake. The sound of the engine would roar across the wasteland as the rpm surged, using compression power to slow down. One could not help but envision what it was like out in this remote place when the spring floods came to power and exercised their authority. Not much of anything could stand in their way. The thought of it made you furtively shoot a glance to their origins in the great mountains on the south horizon just to make sure a wave of water was not coming. We were following the trail of Marco Polo that stretched two thousand five hundred miles across China. It started in Kashgar and finished in the old capital of Chang'An, , Xian, China. It was fifteen hundred miles from Kashgar to the end of the Great Wall of China in the city of Dunhuang. There in Dunhuang stood the final outpost of former Chinese civilization called the Jade Gate.

It was considered the end, not the beginning, because the perspective of civilization looked west from their center in Xian. In fact the Chinese dynasties considered themselves to be the center of the world, calling their country the Middle Kingdom. Beyond the Jade Gate was no man's land, the Taklamakan desert, the place of barbarians and exiles. Along the southern and northern peripheries of the Taklamakan, which is actually an extension of the Mongolian Gobi Desert, were strings of oasis cities connected by camel trails. These were two branches of the Silk Road that joined back together on the western edge of the desert in Kashgar on the Kyrghyzstan border.

The road in many places was still nothing more than a camel trail. Marco Polo had taken the southern route on which I was now traveling towards the city of Khotan. He had written of his stay in that ancient city. Khotan was the source of Imperial Jade for the emperors, and beautiful carpets for all Cathay. Before the invasion of the Communist Chinese, the area was almost exclusively Moslem. Except for the Communist placed workers and officials, the cities were still Moslem strongholds. I was present to bring them the message of Jesus Christ, the living Son of God. As a bonus, I was a beneficiary in getting to do what hardly anyone from our civilization had ever done; follow Marco Polo's entire trek across China.

My fixed gaze on the horizon was rewarded by the sudden emergence from the desert floor of a line of green! The trees were a signal that we were approaching the oasis of Khotan. This was a remarkable sight to behold upon driving out of the desert. On passing the first line of vegetation watered by streams from the Kunlun Mountains, we would enter a paradise standing in vivid comparison with the surrounding parched and roasted wasteland.

Once inside the oasis it was hard to imagine anyone would leave. There were vineyards, wheat fields, and orchards. Khotan was such an oasis, except it grew into a sizable city. It stood on the White and Black Jade Rivers, the source of Chinese jade for millennia. Boulders and rocks of jade would come tumbling down into Khotan out of their source in the mountains, washed in by the gushing spring deluge. The rivers then would run out past the city and totally disappear into the sands.

The jade was never mined, only found in the rivers by the locals who knew how to search in the water with their feet for the precious stones. The same waters provided the lush greenery that was now such a sweet respite from the days of traveling across the great desert. I planned to distribute my literature, rest, and then resume my journey. It didn't take much in those Silk Road towns to draw a crowd. Westerners were rare and an object of curiosity. My Chinese little brother, John Hu, would double as a sentry. If he spied any police or other potential troublemakers he would barge into the crowd and whisk me away. As we drove into the center of Khotan, the Holy Spirit spoke to me and let me know that an American Christian missionary was there who desperately needed my help. I could feel urgency in my spirit as we checked into our little hotel. I told those who were with me that as soon as we had cleaned up, we were going back out. After taking a very needed shower, we went into town.

We got out of our vehicle and a crowd of onlookers formed around us. I passed out tracts of an essay I had written and translated into the local script. At the same time, I used the opportunity to ask if anyone knew of a foreigner working in town as an English teacher. Instinctively I knew that any foreigner living long term out here would have to come as an educator. The locals who gathered around us did not know of any such person living in the area. I continued searching and asking until finally I was tired. We went back to our hotel rooms to take a rest. I lay down, but instead of being able to relax waves of anxiety began to roll over me. Extreme loneliness and despondency overwhelmed me. Tears of sadness and hopelessness trickled down my cheeks. My spirit was experiencing what this other person I had been seeking was going through. I recognized the feelings as the assault of dark demonic forces. These attacks try to overtake those who brave the remote pagan regions of the globe with the healing message of Jesus Christ.

My own soul had been assailed with those same evil spiritual forces when I was in Mongolia. It is hard to fully convey the nature of a spiritual attack. Many people would fantasize the event into a television drama of a ghoulish looking demon physically assaulting the victim.

Instead, the worst attacks are in the realm of the mind and emotion. Inexplicable feelings of doom, depression, or alienation flood the messenger of good news in an attempt to debilitate or devastate. Sometimes the attack is steeped in guilt or remorse over past events and people. This type activity is potentially just as ruinous as a physical weapon. There have been bearers of the message who for the lack of encouragement and edification, have succumbed and literally lost their minds.

It was just such a spiritual weapon that I was sensing. I jumped from my place of rest and told my companions we have to go back and resume our search for the missionary. The process of being directed by God seems mysterious to many. Really, it is very much a process of simple obedience to His promptings and making yourself available. My strategy is to obey His signals, and then allow Him to guide my steps. This is how the supernatural develops into a lifestyle.

We got into our Toyota and headed back into town. I knew a Christian here in one of the most remote cities in the world desperately needed my help and I had to find that person.

In the downtown area of Khotan there were some simple stores selling different kinds of items. I began to walk in and out of them, seeing where I would be led. I entered a small, interesting place that sold Chinese made items. Behind the small counter was a lady shopkeeper attentively watching her store. Overhearing me speak with my companions, she discovered I was from the United States of America. Intent on selling me her wares, she spoke to me in halting English obviously practicing an unfamiliar language. I was astonished as she was the first person knowing any kind of English we had met since leaving Kashgar. Without hesitation, in an amazed tone, I asked her, "Where did you learn your English?" Her simple answer, once articulated, came with the full weight of divine revelation, "From the American teacher!"

"Where can I find this American teacher," I asked anxiously. "She lives at the state school dormitory for teachers," she replied. My pulse and speech quickened with the anticipation of finding the object of my quest. I asked her to take me there but she couldn't leave her business. I spied an antiquated looking rotary telephone on her counter. Taking a wild shot, I asked her to call the American teacher. It shocked me when she said that she would! I didn't at all expect her to be able to call.

The whole situation was developing rapidly and even though I had set out to search for the American missionary, the sudden turn of events was a wonderful surprise. She picked up the old telephone and with her right index finger dialed deliberately. She spoke in Chinese with someone on the other end and handed me the phone. Grabbing the phone I spoke boldly, presuming what the Spirit had revealed to me to be true, but I had no circumstantial substantiation for my purposes. "My name is Larry Garza, I am from the United States and I want to meet the person who has given their life to serve God on the back side of the desert."A feminine voice answered in a tone of desperation, "Come immediately!" My Chinese guide took directions from the shopkeeper, and we were on our way. Our short trip brought us to an institutional looking multi-story building very typical of the remote areas of China. It was gray, drab, and functional. We went to the dormitory section by way of the outside stairs and climbed to the third floor. We then entered into a dimly lit hallway with apartment doors lining both sides. The building was so stereotypical of Communist architecture I could almost walk through it blindfolded. These apartments, or what we would call tenements, are ubiquitous throughout the entire Communist world. They always seem to come with a sparse, worn out playground for the children. All seem to even have the same dank smell of mortar and cement.

I knocked on the door and it opened slowly. There in the doorway stood a thin woman in her fifties. Her ascetic dress was obviously homemade, and even though she was very tidy in appearance, the material was the kind I had seen covering the sacks of flour in the Chinese stores. I wasted no time with salutations but walked in, let her close the door, and I began to speak, "Jesus has sent me here today and He wants you to know you are not alone!"

Immediately her eyes filled with tears and her face contorted with pent up emotion. "Jesus wants you to know your work is not in vain and He is going to supply all of your needs." The atmosphere was charged with the power of God in the small living quarters and the woman released her obvious sorrow with intense crying while holding both hands to her face. Finally, she regained her composure and I recounted to her how the Holy Spirit had let me know about her, and had enabled me to find her. She shared her poignant story with us. She had been out here in the desert without seeing a fellow American for five years. Hers was a life of solitude in that she worked as a missionary and she was the only Christian in the area. She had no one of common spirit to fellowship with her or to share her concerns. To top it off, her supporters in the United States had forgotten about her and sent no mail or finances. Her salary was the meager portion allotted by the Chinese government to teachers they knew were subsidized by their friends back home. So she lived in poverty. Then there were problems with her grown up son who was struggling in every way. Guilt assaulted her as a mother for leaving her son. Evil spiritual forces had obviously used the circumstances to put great pressure on her soul. The feelings of alienation and depression anyone would encounter were only heightened by the desolate landscape. Without anyone to console, comfort, or encourage her, she related that just before our arrival she thought she would lose her mind. Imagine her emotional and spiritual invigoration when she learned how God had supernaturally sent me to her.

God can send you the messenger you need even on the backside of China! It is mind-boggling when you think of the divine orchestration of events it had taken to get to her!

I made a quick mental calculation of the cash I had and what I should need of it to finish my journey. I counted out two hundred dollars cash. As I gave it to her, the look on her face was awesome. Even her financial needs were being met! Two hundred dollars cash was a lot of money as her salary was about fifty dollars a month. What is the best restaurant in town?" I asked. You have to remember we were on the backside of China, not much in terms of eating out!

Nonetheless we made arrangements and that afternoon we took her to the best place in Khotan. During dinner we found out more of her pressing needs and we were able to make arrangements for them to be taken care of.

God had once again guided us supernaturally for His purposes! His sovereignty is not limited by geographical placement! Wherever we are in the world, God knows where we are and can get to us with what we need. Having accomplished this aspect of our mission in Khotan I was greatly relieved of the burden that had been on my soul. Now I felt I could continue with my trek across China.

The city of Khotan held a great fascination for me, as Marco Polo had been here and I wanted to explore it some more. On my first trip to China I had visited the palace in Beijing called the Forbidden City, where the emperors of China had lived for five hundred years. I had been especially impressed with their jade collection. Many people associate jade with the color green but actually green jade has only come into vogue in the last one hundred years. The imperial jade was white, in fact a specific white called mutton fat jade.

This type of white jade is much more rare than green jade. Khotan was the source of the imperial white jade for China since prehistoric times. Marco Polo had documented the jade trade of Khotan while visiting there. In the back of my mind, I wanted to find a good piece for my wife, Linda. The rough stones are found in the two main Khotan Rivers and then shaped and polished by the local lapidarists called "jade doctors." I went down to one of the Khotan Rivers, and looked around but I didn't find any promising piece of potential jade.

Leaving the river, I walked down a tree-lined lane through a neighborhood. A Uighur man sat on a wooden chair on the side of the lane. He was dressed in the traditional modern Moslem costume that one finds men wearing all the way to Turkey. All across Central Asia the men wear an ubiquitous outfit consisting of type of golf hat, sports coat, dress shirt, and long pants. As I walked by with

John Hu he called to us but only John could understand him. I asked John what he was saying. John informed that he was offering to sell us a jade rock in the rough. "Let me see it," I told John. He pulled out from his jacket a flat but large oval jade rock about six inches long.

Jade in the rough is always a gamble because you can't tell exactly what will turn out after shaping and polishing. However, I felt good about this piece. I asked his price and found out he wanted ninety dollars. Bargaining intensely, I was able to negotiate a final price of forty dollars. My next step was to go to the "jade doctor" and get him to cut the shape and design I wanted. I designed a beautiful scene with lovebirds in a Chinese motif, and my wife's name in Chinese characters and in English. After the lapidarist had begun the process, I went to check on my piece of jade. The Chinese jade doctor was very excited. I had found a number one quality mutton fat jade stone worth thousands of dollars in the international jade market! The finished pendant was about three inches long by two inches wide and one quarter deep deep. It was a masterpiece of Jade carving with my wife's name inscribed. Whenever she wears it, and Chinese people see it, they are simply amazed! It is an imperial jade pendant truly worthy of an empress.

I spent my time in Khotan mixing with the people and distributing my translated essay among the locals. It was such a fascinating time that three days just flashed by. My Chinese driver was the brother-in-law of John Hu. He was not a believer in Jesus Christ. We had nicknamed him "Andy" at the beginning of our journey. The Chinese, as many Orientals, have an innate sense of the divine hand of God. They acknowledge divine circumstance when they see it. Day by day my driver would be amazed at the God ordained circumstances taking place. My search for and the discovery of the missionary lady in Khotan had thoroughly astonished him. I had no natural way of knowing the circumstances. The Chinese also recognize fortuitous events, such as my naively purchasing a jade stone worthy of the emperor for virtually nothing, as God given. He had started the journey with me incredulous of the mission of a foreigner. Mile by mile he was being convinced of my relationship with God by the extraordinary series of events taking place before his very eyes. The scriptures frequently refer to the favor of God. The idea of favor is that of a privileged life with divine approval. The driver saw God's favor on my life everywhere we went. It fascinated him as well that I was offering everyone a relationship with God for free. A sorcerer or shaman would charge for the supernatural, but he saw me live it and give it away for free!

One afternoon I took everyone out into one of the Khotan Rivers. It is normally a wide stream but it being summer, the river had separated into different channels now divided by dry rocky riverbeds. We sat down on some rocks and I read from the scriptures in the book of Acts how the disciples had spoken in tongues, a heavenly language only understood by God. Until this time John Hu was a believer as a result of my efforts, but had not entered into the supernatural life available to the Christian.

Out in the middle of the river, with the driver present, I laid hands on John Hu and he began to speak in tongues! Andy worked with him on a daily basis. He was totally beside himself at what was taking place in John's life.

Another incident of divine favor was soon to take place as we left Khotan. It was to be the clincher in his conversion.

When I studied about the Old Silk Road, I found out that the explorer Sven Hedin had discovered the ancient ruins of Khotan in the desert near the modern city. Inexplicably the original inhabitants abandoned the ancient city with many artifacts. The shifting sands of the Taklamakan covered up the town and it became a mystery of time located out in the desert.

For centuries, the local people would venture out across the sands to the ruins and retrieve treasures. I read one account written by a British woman traveler. She described how the simple desert dwellers used precious Ming porcelain retrieved from Ancient Khotan to entertain her.

At the beginning of our journey I had requested of John Hu that we visit the site so maybe I could find an artifact. John Hu and the driver both let me know it was quite a difficult trip by camel to the ruins. "Anyway all of the old things are all gone," John said in a very discouraging manner. I gave up my intentions to visit the archaeological area.

We left Khotan early in the morning and stopped at the edge of town to eat a breakfast of flat Moslem bread baked in an outdoor oven. The clay oven was beside the road on the edge of the desert. It was our launch off point as we left verdant Khotan for the burning sands of the Taklamakan. There was no place to sit so we stood outside our dusty Toyota land-cruiser, munching bread and drinking bottled water. While standing there reflecting on the events that had transpired, I saw a little Uighur man wrapped in his black sheepskin robe and peculiar hat come walking out of the desert with his head bowed. He was absorbed in his own thoughts as he trudged along carrying a very old and frayed burlap sack. I observed him as his route brought him out of the desert onto the dirt track on which our vehicle was parked. He walked onto the road and came slowly toward us. His stiff gait and stooped shoulders revealed the years of hard life spent out in the wasteland. As he walked by me, he looked up and his haggard unshaven peasant countenance came to life when his eyes met mine. You could tell my visage had created an idea that was inspiring him to instant action. Without saying a word, he stopped, set the burlap sack down, stooped and reached deeply into the burlap producing an object swathed in old, dirty rags.

Mindful of my presence, he slowly and carefully unwrapped the object. He unveiled a beautiful old vase covered in archaic style Chinese characters and figures. As if blinded by a sudden flash of light, I tried to adjust my eyes to the totally unexpected vision of the object from ancient Khotan. Keeping my composure, I told John, ask him where it came from. John spoke to him and turning to me said, " He found it out in the desert!" Not wasting time, I retorted, "How much?" Their guttural Uighur conversation seemed to take forever. "One hundred eighty Yuan," was John's answer. My mental calculation of currency rates yielded an approximate amount of about twenty-two dollars. Without even blushing I countered with an offer of ninety Yuan.

We rapidly came to a compromise of one hundred twelve Yuan or about fourteen dollars.

As we clambered back aboard our Toyota Land Cruiser, I was exultant! Andy the Chinese driver was absolutely overwhelmed. For some reason this was the miracle of circumstance that brought him to a belief in Jesus Christ. He had seen John Hu speak in tongues on the Khotan riverbed, but when he saw me receive the object of desire, that was it! Maybe it was because John had said it was impossible. Or, maybe it was the way it was hand carried to me out of the wasteland. Every chance he had, he would take the vase out of the wrapping and pore over it meticulously, holding it with a curious stare. He looked at it as if it might vanish at any moment. It was shortly afterwards that I prayed with him to receive Jesus Christ as his Lord and Savior.

Once again, we were on our way down the Old Silk Road of Marco Polo fame. To retrace his steps is to really learn to respect his accomplishment. At the time I made the trip in 1996 not even National Geographic Magazine had ever had a representative make the journey. To think that Marco Polo did it by camel, what an accomplishment! Marco Polo wrote of men going mad at night on the journey from the screams of demon spirits out in the desert. You would not believe his story from the comfortable vantage point of your couch in your carpeted, climate-controlled, living room.

To go there is to experience the stark spirituality of the terrain. You might be skeptical until you are there on the dirt track of the Old Silk Road, your headlights piercing the blackness, uninterrupted for hundreds of miles by any artificial light. There you too might hear voices or see apparitions!

While traveling through the Taklamakan on a moonless night, the stifling darkness creates a canvas where imagination causes the outlines of passing shapes to merge. Personally, I found it to be an exciting revelry for my soul and senses. Most probably the Taklamakan landscape becomes a mirror for your mind. I think the determinant factor is whether or not your mind is filled with good. If so, you may experience great things from the tableau of the endless sand and rock. It is no place to be if you are ridden with guilt, remorse, or depression. The bleakness would become a screen for the projections of your anxieties with every regret becoming magnified. I know this ability of the Taklamakan to amplify the mind's condition had something to do with the missionary of Khotan almost losing her mind.

The Taklamakan desert has a great beauty, but its aesthetic quality is one of extreme desolation interrupted by oasis habitations. The intensity of effort required in managing the vehicle through the often difficult and dangerous road would frequently wear out Andy, our Chinese driver, and I would take over the wheel for many hours. Actually, I loved driving through the Taklamakan! Feelings akin to that of a great pensive solitude, as if I were on a spiritual retreat, inundated my soul.

Despite the continual presence of my companions, many times I felt totally alone as I drove across the vast expanse while deep in thought. Instead of becoming weary from the grueling drive, I felt continually exhilarated, as if I was on a vigil and the expected epiphany would manifest at any time.

We came upon the most amazing sights while in the wasteland. In places where it seemed impossible that any person could possibly eke out a living, there would be a small group of huts. Sometimes we would come to an absolutely forlorn village where we were supposed to stop for the night and I would make the decision to press on because it felt inhospitable to me. On one occasion I drove for sixteen hours, stopping only after my vision had blurred and my eyes were burning so badly that only sleep could bring relief.

It was on the portion of trail between Khotan and Minfeng that we came to a decent government hotel after many hours of driving. There was only hot water available from a wood fired boiler for one hour, from nine to ten p.m.! We had raced into town arriving just minutes after ten p.m. The inflexible counter lady simply refused to accommodate us with any hot water, as we were too late. She was stereotypical of the Maoist Communist government worker trained in regulations with no sympathy for human need.

I blew up! My fatigue, accentuated by my need for cleanliness, drove me to an exasperation I had never known. I became more adamant than she. I ranted and raved, threatened and cajoled, for the first time in my experience with Maoist officialdom, I won! She relented, ordered her Uighur comrades to disobey government hotel policy and fired up the boiler for an incredible fifteen minutes more! If you have ever experienced Communist officialdom you would know this would be like an American policeman letting you off with a warning for speeding through a school zone! As I ran up the stairs, passing an open stairway window, I could see the wood boiler beginning to smoke. With capitalistic decadence, I jumped in the shower stall and turned on the luxury of hot water! I had just enough time to lather down with soap and rinse one time when the water quit. I dressed and strode down the stairs to meet my fellow travelers, with the air of a great victory about me. It is funny how in the remote places of the globe the most common things of our society take on the importance of world events! Coincidently, John Hu met a friend that he knew that evening in the meager lobby of the Minfeng hotel. He was headed in the other direction, all the way to Kashgar, which really amazed us.

We left Minfeng before dawn the next morning, eager to make it into the ancient town of Quiemo by the end of the day. It was at least two hundred miles of hard driving to Quiemo, so we had an arduous journey ahead of us. Quiemo was a city known for the collection found there of astounding mummies thousands of years old still existing in perfect condition. The original inhabitants of this part of China were actually European looking and were renowned as great horsemen. They buried their dead with a horse head on top to mark the burial site. The desert is so dry the remains were perfectly mummified. I had seen some of the mummies in the state museum of Urumuji. We came in out of the sand and rock into the town of Quiemo and an amazing sight greeted us. For about two weeks we had driven through desert towns and cities with scarcely any evidence of the modern day world. This entire town was being rebuilt at one time! Not only were there buildings being built and painted, but new sewer lines and water lines were being installed as well. Streets were being paved; power and telephones lines were going up. Almost every kind of construction imaginable was visible. On the way to our hotel we stopped at the local bank for John Hu. They had a new computer operating in the lobby! I thought to myself, "What in the world is going on out here on the backside of China?"

We checked into our unusually adequate lodging at the Quiemo Hotel on the fringes of town. Though small and rustic, the lobby had on display their claim to fame, the largest piece of Nephrite Jade in the world. When I was introduced to the manager, I inquired on how it was that the entire town was being rebuilt at one time. He spoke in a thickly accented, but decent English. Only occasionally did he probe John Hu for a word or phrase.

The manager went on to explain the total urban renovation of Quiemo. "You may not know of this but there is a large oil company named Esso," he proudly informed. "They came exploring for oil here some time ago. Last year the Vice President of Esso flew into Quiemo on his private jet and gave us money for the oil rights to this political district. He gave the district of Quiemo seven million American dollars. This is how we have come into our modernization plan." I was astounded, as the outside world knew nothing about this! The major oil company for which I worked for ten years had beaten me here! They, of course, had the right amount of money available. I thought,"If only the believers of Jesus Christ had this kind of world vision to explore, pioneer, and develop the spiritually undeveloped places of the Earth!" "Well, anyhow, I am doing what I can do," was my wistful thought. There in the lobby of the hotel, after speaking with the manager, I was hit with a verbal thunderbolt. I had two Americans traveling with me, Carter Ware and Steve Callies. Steve came up to me in the lobby as we were settling in and said with lowered eyes, " I left all my money in Minfeng!" His quiet voice resounded like a thunderclap in my ears. "I left the seven hundred dollars under my pillow," was his lame excuse. My mind raced through the possibilities; at least two days hard drive to go there and back, surely the money wouldn't be there if we did go back. Maybe there would be unseen entanglements. None of my speculation was promising. Tempted to scold him furiously I decided instead to speak in faith no matter what my emotions were saying. "Everything is still there safe, let's find a way to communicate with Minfeng."

John Hu went to the hotel counter and found out they had a telephone and that we could call Minfeng. Then an amazing series of events took place! The stiff Communist official lady who had given me so much trouble over fifteen minutes of hot water answered the telephone. She went to check the room where Steve had stayed. When she came back, she related that the Uighur housekeeper had found the seven hundred dollars, but since she didn't know what it was she has put it back under the pillow! She had never seen foreign money before!

Then it turned out the friend of John's who was traveling to Kashgar was there at the Minfeng counter at that moment we were calling! John spoke to his friend and for a reward of fifty dollars he agreed to take the money to John's wife in Kashgar. Then John offered to give Steve the same sum of money from his pocket. A catastrophe was averted and three days wasted driving the same section of hard road was avoided!

We spent a full day in Quiemo, resting for the arduous trip into the Tibetan Plateau ahead. I went about meeting people and sharing the message of Jesus Christ. We also took some time and went to look at the graves of the mummies. As of yet, no comprehensive archaeological investigation had been done at the site. Several mummies were just barely under the surface of the sand and visible. The customary horse's head lay on top of them to see them through into the afterlife. Though I was tempted and could have easily done so, I didn't dig up any of them. They were too great a treasure for a rank amateur like me to disturb. I left them for the experts who would certainly come some day.

The next day we left for Roquiang, which was to be the turn off point for us. There in Roquiang we would turn south and ascend from the Taklamakan desert into the Quinghai or Northern Tibetan plateau and down into the basin of that plateau called the Quingdai. We would be leaving the low wasteland and entering the high one. The basin of the Tibetan plateau would be a fascinating place; it is eight to ten thousand feet high, which was low in comparison to the mountains. With nostalgia I was looking forward to finally leaving the beautiful desert. It had been a fantastic experience, but we had been there many days, and it was time to move on. I was relishing our arrival in Roquiang. We drove two hundred miles through the desert into Roquiang arriving in early afternoon. We pulled up to our lodging, but the wretched condition of the inn and town gave me no peace. I took one look at the lodge and barked, "Woemen Zho!" Mandarin for "Lets Go!"

We took off again but on the way out of town we came to a washed out bridge over a dried riverbed. We could see that the road beyond the bridge was impassable. Where we were stopped, two Chinese men squatted by the side of the road, in baseball catcher style, looking quite comfortable in a position that would torture most westerners. John Hu asked them for directions to get back on to the road out of town. They spoke back and forth for a few minutes. Then John turned to me and said, "They say we must drive south on the old river bed until we see the old airplane crashed in the desert sands. There you must go left and go across the dunes until you see the road track."

The directions and the element of chance involved in following them
without mishap challenged my mind. I was conscious of the fact that
there was no other viable option; there was no turning back for us.
"Zho, Zho, Go, Go," I commanded John Hu who was driving. John
put the Land Cruiser into four-wheel drive and we went off the road
and down into the dry riverbed. We proceeded south, using the
boulder-strewn streambed as our road. Our vehicle was on very rough
terrain as we slowly proceeded on the dry riverbed, jostling and
jarring along.

Then our situation really began to complicate, the dry course of
the stream began to split into different directions. Struggling to
maintain control of the wheel as we bounced over rocks and through
washouts, John shouted at me, "Which way, which way!" I broke
out speaking in unknown tongues believing that the Spirit of God
would guide us supernaturally. Interrupting my flow of prayer, I
pointed down one channel of the dried watercourse, and shouted,
"That way!" John heroically wrestled the Land Cruiser in the
direction I pointed, narrowly averting stones and pits that would
have wrecked us. The intensity of my prayer in tongues seemed to
match the tortuous road we were on. Several times we came to a
critical juncture as the riverbed twisted and turned, coming to splits
that determined our course. I stayed in an attitude of prayer, speaking
mysteries to God in my spirit in an unknown tongue. My finger
became the dowsing rod in the hands of God, as I would point to go
in a direction that I had no earthly way of knowing to be correct. My
carnal mind began to fight against my faith, insinuating that we had
lost our way. Suddenly we came to a place where the level of the
riverbed was just slightly lower than its banks and off to our left in
the sands we saw the remains of a crashed DC-3. With a final violent
lurch the Toyota leapt over the embankment and drove smoothly
over sand towards the DC-3. One could only wonder how the airplane
had gotten out here but it was silent as to its past and sat in the sands,
a monument to another era of air travel. As we came up to the wreck
we saw the tracks of the Old Silk Road begin again just as the
squatting men had told us back in Roquiang.

We got back on the road and began settling down from the excitement of our off-road adventure. We didn't know it was training ground for the way ahead of us. We stopped to eat, as we knew many hours of driving were in store for us. I had the Chinese version of Ramen Noodles, the kind you pour hot water on and let sit. The problem was that our Chinese-made thermos only kept the water hot a very short time and all we had was lukewarm water. After pouring the lukewarm water over the dry noodles they would remain crunchy. I barely noticed as the ecstasy of my journey overrode any temporal dissatisfaction.

The fulfillment one experiences in carrying out a missionary expedition is indescribable. Destiny with its mixture of spiritual experience and adventure produces a satisfaction that feeds the hunger of the purposeless modern life. Once tasted it can never be fasted from, only the feast of destiny will do from that time on.

Dusk was descending on the desert behind us as we climbed onto the Tibetan plateau. Now we were in a mountainous desert. The Himalayas condense all the moisture from the seasonal monsoon rains, making the table of the North Tibetan plateau and its mountains extremely dry. The mountain range we ascended was the Altun Shan, a range that runs Northeast of the Kunlun. The road went up diagonally on a mountain without bothering to zigzag. After coming over the peak, we were welcomed by sand drifts that had been blown up against it. They covered the road and were deep in places, making it treacherous to navigate even though we were going straight down again, cutting diagonally across the escarpment. I stopped precariously on the road that seemed more of a ledge chiseled out of the mountain face. John took over, as he was more experienced in driving his vehicle. It was getting dark and visibility was diminishing rapidly. I thought it was quite a feat for us to be descending on such a route.

Astonishingly, a Chinese truck peculiar to that part of the world, very narrow but able to carry high loads, was coming up the road toward us! As they got close, I spied what was obviously a family in the cab. The father driving, a very young elementary school age girl in the middle, and mother in the passenger seat. I was momentarily overwhelmed by their life. We were nowhere, many hours from the last town and there were only perilous obstacles ahead for them to overcome. It was high adventure for me to make the journey in a Toyota Land Cruiser, much less in a cargo truck! My mind's eye can still clearly see the image of their faces, staring out the windshield of the truck cab, coming up that mountain, their top heavy load swaying sideways. We scooted as far as possible to the right, hugging the mountain as the truck passed us dangerously close to the edge. It was a passing commentary on the harshness of family life in China. They squeezed on by us, their stoic faces never showing any concern or even annoyance for making them hazard their lives to get by us. When we came to the bottom of the mountain, we almost drove off an edge that was easily twenty feet from the bottom. It came up so sudden; John hit the brakes, stopping just short of the canyon formed by a stream that ran at the bottom.

This was the end. There was no more road! This time I was at a loss for what we would do.

John Hu backed up our vehicle until he saw a gradual incline that sloped into the streambed below. He descended down into the canyon and drove onto the streambed. I thought the road out of Roquiang would be the only time we would use a riverbed as a road! Except this one had shallow water running in channels. Several times we had to get out and place rocks under the wheels of the Toyota in order to drive on. I kept seeing the image of the Chinese truck family. They had to come this way! How did they do it?

Night fell as we navigated the gorge and it opened into a wide place. Our headlights were the only light and we were in one of the most inhospitable terrains in the world. We were back to navigating our direction by faith in God. There was no marked road of any kind. Only this time the splits in the course of the riverbed were engulfed in darkness of night. Abruptly, the ray of our headlamps fell on an impossible sight.

There, huddled around a battered truck trailer, were many Chinese families. They were squatting down, dirty and disheveled, miserably eating rice with chopsticks out of small bowls. There must have been at least fifty people of all ages, clustered in groups of what looked like parents with their children. We could not help but drive up on them as they were situated in the center of the dry watercourse. A group of the men ran up to us and clustered at our windows. I was apprehensive, as I didn't know where the situation was leading. John spoke in Chinese through his open window for what seemed a long time. He turned to me, informing me that they were a crew of Chinese laborers making a road out here in the wilderness. They claimed their only vehicle had broken down and they wanted to hitch a ride to the next town. I was torn between compassion for their squalid lives and the ever-real danger of a ruse. There really was no room left in our Toyota and I used this as a very good excuse not to chance the experience of robbery or mayhem. They didn't seem disturbed by my denial of their request. Most of the crowd around us went back to the huddles and resumed squatting. Two men remained by John's window and gave him directions on how to get out of the riverbed. We traveled just a bit further and John came to a breach in the bank and we left the all too familiar dry river road.

It was now late evening, and again we began to ascend another mountain by means of a narrow road. As we neared the crest of the peak, the most glorious full moon I had ever seen appeared. The luminous orb slipped past the peak overshadowing us with its massive presence. Our lives took on an ethereal quality as we drove up the mountain with the illuminated lunar landscape seemingly so close. Deceptively my senses told me I could reach out with my hand and touch the moon. It was as if the Tibetan plateau we were on and the terrain of the moon were one and the same, separated only by a short expanse of lake dusted with diamonds.

When I pointed out the night sky to John he told me, " Tonight is the first night of the New Moon festival. I should be with my family but I have chosen to come with you across China."

It was the first day of the New Moon festival, 1996. "I know John," I replied, "This holiday for you is like Christmas for us." "During the New Moon Festival, the whole family gathers and gives gifts, and feasts on Mooncakes!" He beamed at me with a smiling countenance swathed in celestial radiance, while we drove on and on.

We came to a mountain town that seemed more reminiscent of an American industrial city than a remote area of China. It was obvious that there was an industry that dominated the town with its smokestacks and dust. It was after midnight and John was searching for the place we would spend the night. In response to my questions, he was trying to describe the mineral that was mined here. As we came to the shoddy place of stay for the rest of the night, he was grasping for the English word. Finally he resorted to descriptions of the valued ore. "It doesn't burn, and it is used to protect from fires," he described in desperation from lack of the word. I was greatly fatigued but suddenly the realization dawned on me, "Asbestos," I shouted, "No way, we are not staying here!"

I thought of the haphazard Chinese safety measures that surely allowed the entire town to be contaminated with deadly asbestos dust. Andy, Carter, and Steve had been quiet passengers in the back for many hours. Andy did not understand my reason for not wanting to stay, and he was on the verge of mutiny. I didn't care what he thought; I was not staying in a Chinese Asbestos mining town! Steve Callies and Carter Ware were catatonic with fatigue but were trustful of my judgment.

"Zho, Zho, Go, Go!" I said to John. Humbly, John put the car back on the road and we headed across the basin called the Qaidam. It is a high altitude desert with large salt lakes. I took over the wheel as we headed across this eight to ten thousand foot of elevation wasteland. John rapidly went to sleep and I drove on relentlessly in the early hours of the morning.

The crevasses of my earlier experience in the Taklamakan began to reappear, though not as often. This time they lurked hidden in the topography more dangerous than ever. They were more perilous because I was extremely burned out by many hours of hard driving and intense adventures.

It was about seven in the morning when we had started; now it was an hour past midnight. We had been on an action packed hard road for about seventeen hours. My options had left me no choice but to press on. The thought of being asleep, breathing in a cloud of asbestos dust, gave me the creeps.

The hazard now more than ever was that in my fatigue a crevasse would loom up on me, and my reaction time would be too sluggish to slow down properly. If I made a mistake it would be catastrophic. These thoughts ran through my mind, causing me to draw supernatural energy and concentration from a tired out body. Faith has a lot do with extraordinary effort, but will power is just as important. I drove on and on as my companions slept. It was about four a.m. when I finished two hundred miles of road across the Qingdam Basin.

As we came back up onto the Qinghai plateau, my eyes focused on a strange sight. I was driving on the first paved road we had encountered since leaving the outskirts of Kashgar! It was the two-lane highway from Tibet to Dunhuang. I careened wildly as I turned on to the pavement heading north.

For hundreds of miles I had meandered freely on the dirt track of the Silk Road, free to take any side or follow any impulse. Physically wasted, I fought to control the Land Cruiser and keep it in the narrow right lane. I found myself over-compensating, veering from side to side. The narrow highway had a little drop off on each side that produced an even worse effect. I would feel the tires get caught in the gravel then pull hard to get the vehicle back on the pavement.

Then another forgotten experience, a car was coming towards me with its headlamps on! My eyes burned as I tried to focus on the road ahead, blinded by the glare of the lights. Compounding my predicament was the fact the fuel gauge was on empty and we had used up all we had brought with us. It was just before sunrise and I couldn't take it anymore. Exhaustion commanded that I pull over on to the gravel and park. I slept sitting at the wheel and my fellow travelers slept as much as possible in our cramped quarters. It was probably the most uncomfortable sleep I have ever attempted.

The sun shining brightly through my windshield from the morning sky wakened me. We were parked beside a huge oil field filled with many derricks. Our surroundings were reminiscent of a West Texas oil field. John took over the controls again and we took off headed for Dunhuang. Our position was on the highway north of Golmud, halfway to Dunhuang, the Jade Gate. Golmud was an important town at the intersection of two of the ancient routes of Tibet.

Many times on the way here my Chinese companions had called me "lucky." They did so trying to describe the abundant good fortune they had seen occurring for me. I explained to them it was not luck but the blessing of God. For hours I would speak to John Hu from the scriptures on how all believers of Jesus Christ were entitled to be blessed. I would make him repeat after me, "We are blessed!"

We needed a blessing now!

We were out in the dawn of the Qinghai plateau and we needed gasoline desperately. On the left in the middle of nowhere appeared a Chinese mining encampment. The hovels of the miners stood in contrast with the bleakness of the place. We pulled up and I got out of the Toyota. Immediately the miners gathered around me munching on their breakfast of steamed white buns. They were shocked to see me there among them. Excitedly, my tired body came to life as I realized it was a great opportunity to pass out my essay, "Can You Change Your Fate?"

In a loud voice I said, "Wait, I have something for you!" as I motioned from the front seat.

My gesture was too much and they all broke and ran away! John called them all back; reassuring them my intent was good. With a great constraint in motion and voice I handed them all a tract, which they read avidly. John spoke with the manager, telling him of our dire need for gasoline. The manager took us over to a pit where there was a very old oil drum whose cap was secured by a rusty lock. He produced his ring of keys and then proceeded, trying to open it. He struggled, unable to make the key open the unused and corroded lock. Frustrated by his failure, John Hu impulsively grabbed the key from his hand and exclaimed, "We are blessed!" The lock opened up giving access to the greatly needed gasoline. For us it was as important as the parting of the Red Sea! John was jubilant! He kept saying over and over, "We are blessed!" We filled up and headed on to Dunhuang and the Jade Gate, stopping only to eat a simple meal at a roadhouse diner.

Once inside the Jade Gate we were officially in Old Cathay and out of the Moslem area of Xinxiang. Between Dunhuang and the end of the Silk Road is the great city of Lanchow or Lanjou. It was the first truly great modern city we had seen on our journey. I went out on the sidewalk and spent time distributing the essays among the people.

Suddenly, a man appeared and started shouting at me, and a menacing crowd gathered around me. John grabbed me, took me out of their midst rapidly walking me away to a safe location. Andy was there with us throughout the entire tense situation. Their faces were downcast and they seemed unusually subdued. "What is the matter John?" I asked, feeling their incrimination. His eyes lowered, John answered me "The man was shouting, there is no God, this is China, we are Communists! These people are proclaiming the God of the American Imperialists!" John and Andy seemed embarrassed by the event. I felt bad for making them look traitorous to their fellow Chinese. Also, we had been in danger from crowd violence and police arrest. They were my good friends and I wanted God to vindicate the situation. We followed the Silk Road to its terminus in the original capital of Chang An, now called Xian. I remembered that in the seventh century the Chinese emperor had built a stone monument called a stele, to the accomplishments of the first Christians who came to China.

The first Christians missionaries to China, the Nestorians, had followed the Silk Road all the way from present day Mosul, Iraq on camels to the capital of Cathay. There in Xian is a collection of steles that was a royal library.

I was able to find it after some difficulty. I took John Hu, Andy, Carter Ware, and Steve Callies to see the Nestorian monument. When John and Andy saw the Cross of Jesus Christ etched at the top of the stone monument from the year 631 A.D. in China, their countenance illuminated. I told them, "See, there were Christians in China before there was ever an America or Communism. Jesus is for the whole world!"

The age of the monument and that it was written in honor of Christianity by the Chinese emperor greatly impressed them. Veneration and respect for the past runs deep in the Chinese culture. Their helping me to make the journey across China with the message of Jesus Christ took on a new dimension of honor, loyalty, and respect that linked them with Chinese civilization and their elders. John and Andy smiled broadly at me and to each other. John used his favorite American slang term for yes, which he would stretch out to match the degree of his approval, "Yeaaah!"

We had seen notable supernatural events and God's hand had been involved in our lives the whole trip. The journey had been a fabulous accomplishment. We did not break down once or even have a single flat tire! The good fortune of our accomplishment caused John to write a huge banner saying, "We are blessed!" He draped the banner across the front of his Toyota Land Cruiser, announcing our success to all of China as he drove back from Xian to Kashgar by using the paved Northern road.

To this day he tells many people what God did for us on the epic odyssey across China, following in the footsteps of Marco Polo and his ancestors.

I myself will never be able to properly communicate what this journey meant to me as a Christian, as a man, and as a student of history. This chapter only briefly tells some of the highlights. Really,

I am attempting to tell you about my life with Jesus Christ. Some people limit Him to a superficial religious context. Jesus is real and alive. Following Him has caused me to actualize my potential as a man and as a person.

Jesus Christ has exceeded the possibilities I considered of a meaningful life. I have lived many adventures but The Old Silk Road of China was one of the greatest highlights of my life. I have only narrated a few of my adventures experienced in China and Asia.

The only way to summarize that period of my life would be to plagiarize what the Apostle John said in his gospel, "And there are also many other things which Jesus did on the Old Silk Road across Asia, which if they were written in detail, I suppose that even the world itself would not contain the books that would be written!"

You can request a free periodical. Larry Garza can be contacted for information and speaking engagements at the following address.

Larry Garza
C/O
HVM
P.O. Box 421
Dickinson, TX 77539

E-mail address: jmc19@msn.com